Action Hero

A Hollywood to Olympus Romance
Book 5

Elle Rush

Cover by Valerie Tibbs

BLURB

Nobody in Hollywood takes cable television star Glinda Crawford seriously, and that's not going to change with her next movie. What started off as a serious drama has descended into a cheesy flick about rabid, cyborg, panda assassins, and she can't escape the insanity.

Mike Mosley has it all worked out. He's leveraged his teen-age TV heartthrob days into a successful life-long acting career. But the first week on the set of his new movie with his *Olympus* co-star Glinda has him second-guessing everything: the plan, his single status, and just how dangerous robot pandas can be.

When script shenanigans spill into the real world, the attraction Glinda and Mike have been faking turns into a hot, real-life adventure. If they can survive this movie, they can survive anything together. However, the shocking finale surprises them both.

NOTE FROM THE AUTHOR

I adore the *Sharknado* movies. I mean I really love them. For pure entertainment value, they can't be beat. It takes a certain sense of humor to properly appreciate them, but I think they are nothing but fun. Come on! Somebody said, "let's put sharks in a tornado" and then they did it four more times! They even have a spin-off series.

This book is in honor of Ian Ziering, Tara Reid, Anthony C. Ferrante (director), Thunder Levin (writer) and the geniuses at The Asylum, who have taken hilarious absurdity and turned it into fun and profits. This is my love letter to them. And to Steve Guttenburg of the *Lavalantula* franchise, who has been dealing with insane Hollywood scripts before sharknados even existed.

Honoring the realism provided by *Sharknado*, I have taken massive liberties with how movies are made. Because, as they have demonstrated, there is no reason to let facts interfere with a good story.

ACKNOWLEDGEMENTS

I have a lot of people to thank for this book:

Valerie Tibbs, for her great cover, Dayna Hart, for her edits and suggestions, Ross, for suggesting even more panda-monium, Susan Hayes, for her encouragement and prodding, and all my Chatzy girls, for their support, suggestions, and general bad influences.

CONTENTS

Two months earlier

Prologue

It looked like a war zone. Mostly because it was a war zone.

Olympus was in the midst of a battle for the ages, and nobody was sitting on the sidelines. Eros had picked up an axe from a fallen warrior and was fighting like a madman after the death of his beloved Psyche. Athena battled Poseidon with some fancy sword-work, and she, Aphrodite, was facing off against Hera, queen of the Greek gods.

Glinda Crawford towered over Layla Andrews, the diminutive actress who made Glinda's five-foot-four frame look tall. Layla had a short sword and was advancing just as they'd rehearsed when a piece of black plastic the size of her head fell between them. Both women froze, then slowly looked up.

The yelling and clanging on the set had covered the sound of one of the spotlights breaking away from its fixture. It dangled by a cord, banging against the catwalk and raining bits of casing down on them.

It swung like a pendulum again, this time tearing down the light beside it. Glinda tracked the direction.

She didn't have time to yell a warning. It wouldn't have been heard anyway.

She spun on her heel and hiked her toga to her knees in one fluid motion. Two steps got her to the top of the massive marble table in the middle of Olympus's great hall. Two more took her to the end of it. She bent her knees and launched herself forward with all the strength she could muster.

There was no sound. Everything faded away until all that was left was a laser focus on her target. Mike Mosley never saw her coming. Her shoulder hit his waist, knocking him sideways, away from the column he was using for cover before he stabbed Eros in the back. Her momentum pushed them both forward, driving Mike to his knees. She tightened her grip, her other arm wrapping around him from the other side, and rolled him over top of her to move him farther away.

Over all the noise, she heard his distinctive baritone. "What the hell?" he yelled.

Just as the pair of lights crashed into the pillar.

What was left of their casings shattered, taking the bulbs with them, which triggered a secondary explosion. Glass, plastic and metal blasted across the stage, halting everyone in their tracks.

At first, Glinda thought she'd simply knocked the wind out of herself. Then, as she lay atop Mike with her chest pressed against his, she realized she had a problem. "Are you okay? I hit you hard."

"You'll never play defense for the Jets, but you got the job done. Are you okay?"

The strap of her toga, which was supposed to be over her shoulder holding the draping garment together, was half-covering Mike's face. If she moved, she was going to be flashing to cast and most of the crew. "Not really. Be still. If either of us move, my girls will be forever immortalized on screen. If I wanted nude pictures out there, I would have done it already." As the adrenaline burned off, she began to get feeling back in her body. Glinda slowly tightened the muscles in her back, preparing to grab her torn costume, when a bolt of pain shot through her ribcage. "Ow."

"What?"

"I may have cracked a rib or two saving your life."

"You think you saved my life?" A huge chunk of the pillar shifted, then slid to the ground. Seconds later, the column slowly toppled over, landing exactly where Mike had been standing. "Okay then."

Chapter One

Present Day

When she discovered her supper reservations were at the Limelight, Glinda Crawford knew exactly what was happening. She was going to be fired. Her agent only suggested Hollywood's premiere restaurant for very good or very bad news, and Glinda didn't have any career-expanding prospects on the horizon.

The last she'd heard, Fiona had been in negotiations for a two-year contract extension on *Olympus*. Since two recurring characters had already been killed off in the first eight episodes of the season, and the latest script had offed another goddess and a third recurring character, things weren't looking good for Aphrodite.

If it was bad news, Glinda was going to need the oysters. The oysters and the spinach salad and the six-ounce Filet Mignon with the baked potato. And another Cosmo. She might not get back to the Limelight for a while.

She spread the stiff linen napkin across her lap and wrapped her fingers around the stem of her martini glass, sloshing some of her drink on the matching white tablecloth. "Hit me with it, Fiona. Do they not want me back? Are they downgrading Aphrodite to a recurring role? Oh, God, are they killing me?"

Fiona Marshall raised her eyes to the ceiling as if in prayer. "Did we have an espresso this afternoon after shooting finished, Glinda? Because we talked about you having coffee late in the day. You know it turns my hair white."

Fiona's short, white spikes were a fashion statement, despite any claims that they had been caused by Glinda on a caffeine high. Her agent had already been sporting them when Glinda had signed with her nine years earlier.

She had to admit Fiona had been an excellent agent; she'd kept Glinda working constantly. Her first role at twenty-one had been playing a flaky fifteen-year-old human in a vampire high-school series. Then she moved on to a figurative and literal space cadet on a sci-fi show which only lasted one season. When Fiona sent her to audition for a dumb blonde love goddess on a cable series, neither of them expected things to take off like they had. Aphrodite had been her most successful role to date, but it looked like her four-year employment streak was about to come to an end.

And she'd only had one espresso that afternoon. And a half.

The waiter stopped at their table to refill their water tumblers and drop off their appetizers. Glinda sighed after the first oyster slid down her throat. The Limelight's chefs made losing her contract almost worth it.

"Let's talk about why you think you're being fired," Fiona suggested.

"The show hasn't renewed my contract for the fifth season yet. This year has been one big blood-bath. They're obviously planning a major cast shake-up. If they wanted me back, I should have had an offer by now." Glinda loved *Olympus*. She didn't want to leave. The people she worked with were a riot and, despite the intense work schedule, pranks ran rampant on the set to keep things loose.

The quality of the writing had improved since the first year as well. They'd introduced several new characters this season, and a three-sided war between two factions of the gods of Olympus and the mortals gave her character more to do than simply drop one-liners and interfere in other characters' love lives. Aphrodite was still a meddlesome, thoughtless woman, but now she had more to scheme about.

"I sent you an email days ago. They want another two seasons from you. Have you not looked at your phone?" Fiona plucked a bun from the basket on the table and tore a piece off. "I also asked if you wanted to do more fan convention appearances. I was going to bring it up tonight since you hadn't responded."

Glinda called up the e-mail app on her phone, but it showed nothing from either Fiona or her assistant. In fact, it didn't show any new messages from them for the last two days. Glinda closed her eyes. She should have noticed. What else had she missed? "Damn it. My phone hates me. You've got my full attention now. What did they say?"

"They want you. But that's not why I needed to see you."

"It's not?" What more could there be? "Wait! Are you dumping me now that you set me up for two more years? Do you not want me as a client anymore? I thought we worked well together. We're both making money. Am I too old for you? Are you replacing me on your roster with one of the *Sex Inc.* girls?" She was only thirty, pushing thirty-one. In Hollywood that meant she was at the peak of an actress's use-by date. Youth was profitable; thankfully, Glinda could still pass as being in her early twenties. But *Sex Inc.* was a freshman show that had the town buzzing, and some of the cast couldn't legally drink yet. She couldn't compete with that.

"No more coffee for you after noon," Fiona ordered. "I'm not dumping you. I'll happily and profitably take a solid actress on my client list over a one-hit newbie."

"Are you sure you won't change your mind?" The fear of rejection was never far from her mind.

"Will you cut that out? I want you. In fact, I have a new opportunity for you. You've been telling me you want to get into movies ever since Chris Peck did *Three Date Rule* last year during your hiatus."

Glinda jerked so hard, her third oyster slid off its half-shell. "Yes. Of course, yes. You know I've been dying to get into movies. Is it DTV?" Direct-to-video was exploding in new and exciting ways since the cable market had decided there were no limits, but she'd prefer the big screen.

"No, it's a theatrical release. How do you feel about Antonia Caruso?"

Glinda wanted to marry the director's last movie and have little film babies with it. Antonia Caruso had put out four heart-breakingly beautiful dramas in the last twenty years. There was no chance any script she touched would have a two-dimensional, bubble-headed role. Glinda would play a character that only appeared in a handful of scenes to work with such a talented director. "I like her work."

"Good, because her daughter is directing a film. Antonia will be executive producing. She wants you for—"

"Fiona, the best agent in the whole of Southern California, you look lovely."

Glinda didn't need to turn around to identify the speaker. She'd known *of* Mike Mosley since she was a kid, and she'd worked *with* him on and off for the last four years. But Dionysus, the god of fertility, wine, and the arts—or as his fans put it, sex, wine, and rock and roll—had not yet fallen to any of Aphrodite's matchmaking schemes, so she didn't know him well.

It was a shame. He was a tall drink of water. In his late thirties, he'd matured past the college boy look. And he'd done it well. His fit frame rippled under his crisp, white shirt, which also highlighted his dark skin and deep, brown eyes. Mike was one of the most experienced actors on the *Olympus* set; he'd been acting since he was literally in diapers. She had no idea why he was interrupting her business dinner.

"You're late, Mike. Sit," Fiona said.

Until Mike reached for a chair, Glinda hadn't given any thought to the fact they were at a table for four, not two. "Is he joining us?"

"Fiona asked me here for a meeting. I had no idea anyone else would be here. Hello, Glinda. You look lovely, as usual." He sat beside her, and diagonally across the table from the woman who'd set them both up. "What's going on?"

"Glinda's been offered a leading role in a new Caruso movie."

"Antonia Caruso? That's incredible. Congratulations." He meant it. Mike always acted as a cheerleader when anyone he knew got good news. He'd even sent Chris Peck a fruit basket when Chris landed his movie role; it consisted of penis-shaped fruit spears, but it marked the occasion.

"Lucie, Antonia's daughter," Fiona corrected.

"I'll bet she's as talented as her mother. I'm sure you'll be in good hands," he added gallantly.

"She wants you as well, Mike."

That's where his calm demeanor shattered. His jaw dropped. "Excuse me?"

His shock made Glinda feel a little better. Fiona had obviously decided to spring the news on him the same way she'd done it to her.

"Lucie Caruso wants to work with both of you as a package deal. She's a fan of the show and thinks you two have untapped potential chemistry. The question becomes, do you want to work with her?"

"Yes." Glinda couldn't ignore the opportunity. A theatrical release with a Caruso at the helm? It was an early Christmas present to herself.

"What's the script? What's the budget? Who else is involved?" Mike asked.

Trust his logic to burst her bubble. She should probably give those things some consideration.

"A veterinarian studying endangered pandas discovers they've been infected with an incurable virus and creates a cure to save them from extinction," Fiona said.

Glinda closed her eyes for a moment. She pictured herself as a blonde Sigourney Weaver a la "Gorillas in the Mist", only with a Chinese setting rather than an African one. Lush green scenery, a heroic doctor battling to save an adorable yet doomed species. She could imagine exactly how it would play out. Then, remembering her luck, she opened one eye and stared at Fiona. "Mike would be the vet, wouldn't he?"

"Is that a problem?" he asked.

"Not if you don't mind playing the pretty little wife or girlfriend whose sole purpose is to stand around looking pretty while supporting her man. If she's very lucky, she might get to do something stupid to put herself or someone else in danger and need to be rescued."

He nodded at her recitation of the standard leading lady package. "Yeah, that's not a lot of fun," he agreed. "But it could be worse. You could be the big, black bodyguard who has to sacrifice himself to protect the great white savior."

He spoke like he'd had as much experience with his stereotypes as she'd had with hers. "Point."

Fiona, on the other hand, frowned at both of them. She ordered another gin and tonic after the waiter took Mike's dinner order. "I can't believe you two think I'd set you up for parts like that. Yes, Glinda, Mike is the panda doctor. But I promise, you are nothing like a damsel in distress."

"Rival scientist?" Glinda guessed.

"Black market panda procurer?" Mike offered.

"Traveller from the future sent back to save the species?"

"Panda shapeshifter?"

"Oh, good one," Glinda said.

"You're the bodyguard," Fiona interrupted before they could get really imaginative.

"Whose bodyguard?" they both asked.

"The panda doctor's."

Not being the damsel in distress? That was something Glinda could work with. "Still in."

Fiona's smile returned. "Mike's right. You should read it before you commit. I promise you, it's a feature film, but it doesn't have a blockbuster's budget. Obviously, I think you should do it, or I wouldn't have brought it to the table. But as I said, it's the two of you or nothing, so you both need to agree."

Glinda shared a look with Mike. "Give us the scripts."

Chapter Two

According to his doctor, Mike should be starting his day with a kale smoothie and an egg-white omelette. Forty was only two years away, and his metabolism wasn't what it used to be. Instead, he skipped the kale, poured a glass of skim milk, had the egg-white omelette, and tossed a couple turkey sausages in the microwave. He'd throw three strawberries on his plate and call it a balanced meal.

His supper the night before had been much better. He'd cut Limelight's prime rib with his fork. His baked potato had a crispy skin from being tossed in olive oil before it went into the oven, and the fresh butter and coarse sea salt made the flavor explode in his mouth. Mike had pushed the freshly steamed broccoli out of the way. He'd been celebrating.

As an actor, he'd had a good run. Most went years without a permanent job. He'd been working since birth. Babies didn't get a lot of screen time, but he'd had his fair share. Next he moved to an educational kids' show, then a family drama. As soon as he was old enough, he started acting full-time on a college drama.

Most recently, he'd played an FBI agent for six years before that series ended and he'd landed on *Olympus*. Dionysus had started as a recurring role, but he had become a full cast member last year. After almost four decades, he'd done damned near everything.

When he'd asked Fiona to keep an ear out for other opportunities, he hadn't seen this coming. Fan conventions? Sure. Becoming the face of Nikolai cologne? It wasn't an acting job but it paid well. A feature film? That had never even been a consideration. Nobody had considered him for the big screen before.

He thought the same about Glinda. She was a sweetheart to work with, but no one would guess by looking at her that she had the brains or stamina to make it as an actress. She had a lot of curves, and distracting bedroom eyes at every hour of the day, but she'd never taken a serious role in her life. Others could say what they would, but Mike knew her to be a complete professional; she always had enough in her for one more take or to help one of her cast mates. He'd enjoy working with someone like that one-on-one, especially on a project like *The Bamboo Mountain*.

"When you said, 'she thinks Glinda and I have untapped chemistry', were you talking about Antonia Caruso or her daughter?" he'd asked Fiona on their way out of the restaurant. He always felt there was more possible between Dionysus and Aphrodite than their limited on-screen interactions had allowed, but he hadn't realized others had noticed their potential too.

"Lucie. She's a fan of the show. Look, read the script and get back to me by the end of the weekend. They want to move quickly as soon as casting is set."

He'd taken his copy and read it overnight. Now it was spread open on his breakfast bar, waiting for a second inspection. At first glance, it looked good. Better than good. His character, Doctor Montgomery Hanzel, was a world-renowned veterinary virologist brought into a Chinese panda bear sanctuary to solve a deadly outbreak among the endangered species. Jane Mackenzie was an army officer in charge of the proprietary U.S. government equipment he'd brought with him. The script itself was formulaic enough, but the character development made it all work. He was surprised by how much he wanted the part.

He called Fiona to let her know he was in. That's when she dropped her bomb.

"Glinda hasn't called me back yet. I'm sorry, Mike, but it's both of you or nothing."

There had to be a mistake. Glinda wanted the movie from the outset. More than he did. And he wanted it a lot. He hadn't seen anything objectionable to her character. "Can I talk to her? Will you give me her number?" It was just like when he was a kid; if he couldn't have something, it only made him want it more.

"I can't do that, but if you give me permission, I can pass on yours."

"Do it."

He settled into the hammock that occupied much of his balcony and began his third read-through. He concentrated on the dialogue. It was passionate, but there wasn't a lot of humor to it. Then again, being surrounded by dying animals wasn't a very funny situation.

His phone rang just as Hanzel and Mackenzie hit the black moment.

"Do you have any idea what time it is?" the voice at the other end of the line asked.

"Glinda?"

"Mike? I thought I was calling Fiona. She sent me a text and told me to call the number."

He laughed into the phone. He couldn't help himself. She sounded so confused. "I asked Fiona to send you my number. I'm hoping you'll meet me to discuss the script."

"Oh, the script. I'm not awake yet. It's only…" He heard fabric rustling, then a gasp. "Eight in the morning. Are you not aware this is our day off? What kind of monster are you?"

"How about if I buy you breakfast?"

It took some time for her to consider his offer. "Okay, but it had better be a good one."

"The best. I promise."

Ninety minutes later, he was on the north side of Twin Palms Terrace, which offered fresh air, indirect sunlight, and coffee that kept mortal men awake for days.

Mike was concerned when Glinda ordered a second pot.

"I read it. I like it. It's got heart," she said.

He agreed with her verdict. "It's also a small movie, has barely any cast except us, and is relatively low budget."

"Yep." Then they thought some more. The quiet between them was peaceful.

"I need a movie like this," she said unexpectedly.

"Need?"

"I've never been offered a role where my IQ hits triple digits. To play a character who has more to offer than her bra size." Her sigh held more than physical exhaustion. "Captain Jane Mackenzie is smart and competent. She holds a useful role in society. I want people to see me like that. I need that."

He didn't know Glinda well, but he understood the desire to stretch her acting wings. He didn't have a chance to respond before she continued. "I think you and I would work well together. I mean, we already do, but for the most part, this movie would be just us and some pandas. That alone would make it worthwhile," she added with a grin. "But looking at this from strictly a business point of view, it's iffy."

Mike flipped his script over and pulled a pen from his pocket. After he drew a line down the middle of the back cover and labelled the columns "Pro" and "Con", he looked up. "Pros?"

"Strong script. Good co-stars we know we'll get along with. Pandas," she listed.

"Antonia Caruso will take an interest in her daughter's career."

"A con is that Lucie Caruso is a first-time director banking on her mother's reputation."

"Pros include full studio backing and marketing, even for a quieter film like this. Short shooting schedule."

"But no star power beyond us to market it, and the budget reflects that. We'd make more money doing three or four fan conventions over the hiatus instead," she argued.

"Nobody but us will suffer, either." Neither of them had significant others or children depending on them to fill the income gap that came with a hiatus, or had to use the downtime to make up for relationships that took second place during hectic filming periods.

The sun shifted as they worked on the list. Glinda pulled out a pair of pink-framed sunglasses and ignored the stares she got from other restaurant patrons.

By the time they were finished their list, both columns were full and their coffee cups were empty. Glinda declined a third refill, then slumped in her chair after the waitress left. "We're back where we started."

"Money or ego. We shouldn't have to pick." But he'd already made his decision. Ego would win this round. He had a blank spot on his awards shelf, and Caruso films brought home the hardware. It would be a terrific way to close a career. "It all depends on what we want to do. I want this. It's a good part. Not to mention, I'll get to wear pants. I miss pants," he joked. After four years of togas, he was up for expanding his wardrobe choices.

"I miss pants too."

"I guess we've decided. To pants." He raised his water tumbler.

"To pants!"

Chapter Three

She pulled back the curtain and stared down the street for the fifth time in three minutes. Her sister was late. Ten minutes late, but when they only had two days to catch up on three months' worth of news from home, every second counted.

Glinda had offered to pick her up from LAX, but her slightly-older sister insisted she'd be fine using a private car service at the airport. Glinda had arranged one for her; she wasn't going to let Dorothy pay for it on an Iowa teacher's salary.

Eleven minutes.

A navy town car rolled up the street. Glinda didn't hide her excitement. She flew out the door and was waiting on the sidewalk before it pulled up to the curb. "You're late."

"A wizard arrives precisely when she means to."

God, she'd missed Dory.

Per usual, her sister travelled with a carry-on and a medium-sized purse. Glinda knew she had two changes of clothes in the small bag and enough make-up and accessories to go from day-time casual to night-time glam without having to raid Glinda's stash. Her incredible packing ability was only one of the things that made Dory a wizard.

"Come in. Brunch is waiting. I didn't want you to have to wait until lunch since you had such an early start."

"What have you got?"

The question wasn't as simple as it sounded. "Fruit salad, Greek yogurt, and low-fat bran muffins with a few different, organic nut-butters to taste-test."

"Sounds yummy, sis."

Her twin looked good. Clear eyes, glowing skin. Dory's brown hair was cut pixie-short, but it looked healthy. She'd always been taller than Glinda, but over the last year she'd put on some hard-earned muscle which had turned her stick-thin frame into something that didn't scream "I'm a recovering bulimic."

Dory's eating disorder first appeared in high school. Too many thoughtless people making too many thoughtless comments about how twins should be the same size had beat down the poor teenager. Never mind the fact that they were fraternal twins, not identical, and that Dory had six inches on her fourteen-minutes-younger sister. Busybodies insisted that they should be the same weight, and the constant pressure bent Dory to their will. She'd tried to match the numbers on Glinda's scale, which had been stupid. Glinda told her so, but it had taken a hospitalization and a great psychiatrist before Dory had accepted that, twin or not, she was free to be an individual.

Half a lifetime later, Glinda still worried about her. When Dory had agreed to come out to L.A., Glinda made a special trip to the grocery store to stock up on everything healthy. She wasn't going to give Dory any excuses to backslide. Just to keep it from looking too obvious, she also had a carton of Pure Vanilla ice-cream, the stuff with twenty-two percent milk fat, in the freezer, a new bottle of chocolate syrup, and a fresh jar of maraschino cherries in the fridge. In case they stayed in.

"You painted the living room again."

Glinda had forgotten about the change already. She'd done it six months ago, moving from bright white with a teal accent wall, to sage green throughout the room. "Bold contrasts are on the way out."

"You like teal."

She shrugged. Fashion was fleeting and paint was cheap. As vices went, home décor trends were low on the list.

"Did you at least keep the furniture? I loved that furniture."

"I moved most of it into the spare room. Want to see?" Fashionable or not, she couldn't bear to part with the cute end table or the trio of bright blue picture frames. The color wasn't as vibrant against the soft yellow walls as it had been against the white, but Glinda didn't want her guest room to feel stark. She liked the warmth she'd created.

"Oh, very nice." Dory dropped her purse on the bed. "I'll sleep here. Now feed me."

Despite her dark hair and eyes, Dory burned just as badly as Glinda did in direct sunlight, so Glinda pointed her sister at her collection of sun hats and waited for her to make a selection before moving them to the pool deck. Clumps of never-used fresh herbs lined the walls, adding color to the concrete patio blocks.

"Are you sure you want to do this movie?" Dory asked, munching on a pineapple spear. "You'll be on your own most of the time. You won't have anyone around to look out for your interests."

"I've been doing just fine for eight years, Dory. I'll have Fiona. And Mike. I trust him." She didn't doubt her own good guy radar. Nonetheless, she'd grilled Fiona up and down about things she might not have known about her *Olympus* co-star. His Nikolai cologne campaign had come as a shock. Fiona told her the new advertising promotion was launching in a couple months to ramp up for Christmas sales. Unsurprisingly, their mutual agent had only good things to say about him.

"They're going to try to take advantage of you."

"Of course they will. That's why I have a non-negotiable no-nudity clause. I only play stupid, remember?"

"I know that. Now that we've established that I'm okay and you're okay, let's get down to it. Tell me about your hunky Greek god."

"Mike's not my Greek god," Glinda protested.

It took two hours of Mike talk to convince Dory she meant it.

Chapter Four

The box of frozen veggie burger patties on the counter wasn't funny. It would have been hilarious if somebody hadn't written his name on it. It had been too long since he'd used his grill, and now that he was, he refused to waste the opportunity on fake meat when real beef was on the table. The steak at the Limelight had permanently cured him of tofu cravings, not that he'd ever suffered from them before.

"Grab the platter, would you, Mike?" Trent Vaughn ordered on his way through the sliding patio door. "If I accidentally drop the burgers, only my sister and Caitlin will cry."

Trent and Vanessa had been the last people to arrive. Mike's father was already warming up the barbecue after angling the television so they'd have an unobstructed view of the screen when they were on the balcony. They were an odd crew: his dad, a freshly-retired firefighter, Trent Vaughan, a Navy vet trying to reintegrate into civilian life after an injury ended his military career, Trent's sister Vanessa, his *Olympus* co-stars Sean Glenn and Caitlin Kelly, and Rio Rodrigues, who'd played his FBI protégé on his last series. But the thing uniting them could not be denied.

"Hurry up, Mosley, it's the bronze medal match."

The U.S. beach volleyball championships were being televised from Florida.

"Thanks for inviting us," Sean said as he filled a bowl with potato chips. "Caitlin was going to make us watch anyway."

"I know you're both fans. Besides, your cousin is a reigning champion. How could I not?"

"What about Rio?"

"He introduced me to the sport," Mike said. "He was dating a player at the time."

"Excuse me, I was engaged to a player at the time," Rio interjected. "A pro beach volleyball player who taught yoga in her down time. Rachel was awesome."

"And very bendy, from the sounds of it," his dad said.

"That was part of the awesome." Rio swiped a handful of Sean's chips. "But mostly the awesome was her."

Mike placed the platter of steaks beside his dad and took a second to elbow him in the ribs. Rio's engagement had ended ugly a few months earlier. It hadn't been substance abuse or cheating or any of the usual other excuses. Rachel had been struck by a drunk driver while she was biking. Rio had suffered through his bereavement in full view of the press. His friends, like Mike, tried to provide opportunities to get together without having to relive the events again. Right now, Mike's dad wasn't helping.

He shot a look at Sean, who was also aware of Rio's situation. The god of love might be a renowned prankster on set, but he had the best social situational sense Mike had ever come across. He could turn conversations on a dime without the other person realizing what had happened. "Good burger, Mr. Mosley," Sean said after his first bite. "I still overcook mine."

"Call me Joe. Damn right it's good. I'd been barbecuing for a decade before you were even a twinkle in your parents' eyes. And I was a firefighter. I've forgotten more about flames than you'll ever know." His dad's head gleamed with sweat, despite the bandana hanging from his back pocket. It was a sad reminder that men in his family went bald, not gray.

"I hope you know I'm going to want another burger."

"Get your lady one first," Joe ordered. "We're all gentlemen."

Mike gave Sean a nod to thank him for the distraction, then turned the conversation again. "I wonder who they hired as caterer. I can guarantee their food isn't going to be this good," Mike said. Yes, he was biased, but nobody cooked as well as his father. The man was a grill master.

"You'll find out when you get there. When do you start filming?" Sean asked.

"We leave for Hawaii on Tuesday."

"How's Glinda? I know she's always up for a joke on set, but I don't know her that well."

"Fine. I saw her making a list of tourist sites to hit while we were in Honolulu. I don't think we'll have time for any of them, but she is organized like you wouldn't believe."

"Really?"

"She has lists of lists. I saw her phone once."

"How long are you going to be there?" Sean asked.

"We'll be in the islands for a week, but only part of that is on Oahu. I'm anticipating lots of pineapple."

"Probably less than you'd imagine," Vanessa said. She sidled up to the barbecue. "Hey, Mr. Mosley, could you please do a couple veggie burgers next?"

"Sure, darling."

That was love. His father hated to cook veggie burgers, but he adored Trent's little sister. Joe had tried to set Vanessa up with him more than once because "such a pretty girl deserves a good man." Mike had shut him down repeatedly, not because Vanessa wasn't a gorgeous, black woman, but because their dozen-year age difference was something he couldn't get over.

"Rio, come get these ladies a plate."

Now it looked like his dad had another future boyfriend for Vanessa in his sight.

"Will you get any kind of break when you get back?" Sean asked.

"Yeah, a couple days. Which is good, because Martine has us doing *Olympus* promo on *After Dark*, since the new season starts airing in a couple weeks."

Trent tended to ignore their business chatter but his head swivelled over his shoulder at Mike's announcement. "*After Dark*? You're going to be on Johnny Chung's show? That is so cool." The Korean comedian's late-night talk show had ranked in the top three since it had premiered the same night as *Olympus*.

"Do you want tickets?"

"Hell, yes!"

"I think I can do that. Remind me, okay."

"Count on it," Trent said.

Chapter Five

Glinda whimpered. She couldn't help it.

The jumbo jet hit another air pocket, causing it to drop, and Glinda smacked her palm over her mouth. She must not throw up. Again. She'd already used her air sickness bag, as well as Mike's.

They still had another four hours to go.

She didn't understand. This wasn't a tiny, little commuter plane that bounced if a butterfly flapped its wings. Shouldn't they be blowing right through what the flight attendants kept calling "light" turbulence?

A warm hand wrapped around her free one, which wasn't exactly free. It was clenched around the skinny armrest handle. Mike carefully peeled her clawed fingers off the grip, avoiding her crimson-painted nails, and pressed an unwrapped candy into her palm. "It's ginger. It should help with the nausea."

It was an incredibly thoughtful gesture.

It only made her feel worse about what she'd done to his shoes.

But she expected nothing less from him.

In the last couple weeks, Glinda had glimpsed sides of Mike that she'd never seen before. None of them surprised her. After they signed their contracts, it had been a whirlwind of wardrobe fittings and all the other unglamorous things that never made it in front of the camera. He was the most patient man she'd ever met. He didn't blink an eye at any of the numerous delays that came up, and there had been several.

"I guess you're really regretting having to switch seats now, aren't you?" he asked.

Ignoring the upheaval in her stomach, she tucked the candy between her teeth and ground out, "Why? Do they have bigger barf bags in first class?"

At their first video meeting, Lucie Caruso told them *The Bamboo Mountain* would film outdoor scenes in the jungles of Hawaii, which was filling in for southeastern China, before they'd return to Los Angeles to shoot the rest of it. Then she had been a no-show at the airport. She linked in from Europe just before take-off and informed them they'd be dealing with a second-unit director once they arrived in Hawaii, but she promised to be in L.A. for the start of primary shooting.

Glinda thought spending a week in Hawaii sounded like heaven.

She hadn't expected that she'd actually have to die to get there.

She and Mike had started the trip with a pair of seats in first class for the five-hour flight to Honolulu. But when they got to the gate, they discovered the airline had overbooked the flight. It was coach or nothing, and with crew waiting for them at the other end, they couldn't afford a day's delay. They were stuck in the back row of the plane, with seats that didn't recline, next to the toilets.

The plane dropped again, snapping Glinda's jaw closed with enough force to split the candy.

"Kill me now," she begged.

She heard Mike rustling around beside her. She couldn't see what he was doing because her eyes were closed; she could only handle so much input, so she'd cut the visual. "I understand if you want to move."

He took her hand again. She had to open her eyes to see what he put in it. "What's this?" she asked, her fingers clenching around the blister pack.

"Over-the-counter air sickness medication. Guaranteed to work in thirty minutes or less."

She popped two pills through the tin-foil packaging and dry swallowed them before he had time to say another word.

"Can you keep them down?" Mike asked.

"I'll die trying."

He wrapped his fingers around hers and squeezed gently. "Breathe in through your nose and out through your mouth. Nice and slow."

He was being so nice. She closed her eyes again, inhaling and exhaling with his instructions. She heard him tell the flight attendant they didn't need anything, and kept breathing. The plane stopped rocking for more than thirty seconds in a row, and the calm gave her time to get her stomach under control.

"I think I may fall asleep."

"Go for it."

Glinda didn't remember drifting off. All she knew was that she awoke with a warm arm around her shoulders, a rock-hard chest under her cheek, and a sexy-as-hell voice whispering in her ear. "Glinda, it's time to wake up."

She didn't want to.

"Glinda, we've landed."

That, she wanted. "I guess I slept?" She must have. She had no memory of Mike draping his suede jacket over her lap.

"Yeah. Don't worry. I told everyone I was the one who was snoring."

She snorted. She'd never snored in her life. "Thank you. You are a prince among men." Another thought struck her. "Shit."

"What?"

"We still have another flight." They needed to hop a commuter plane to take them to Hilo. The shoot was far away from any civilization which could interfere with the imaginary "remote" location.

Glinda didn't know if she could do it again.

She also didn't know why he was laughing. "You've been asleep for almost seven hours. And can I say when you were out, you were really out." He reclaimed his jacket and slipped it over his tight, black t-shirt. "We had more turbulence due to a wicked head wind. We were an hour late. Then there was some tower traffic and we had to circle for another half hour. We missed our connection."

"Thank God!"

Their first breath of freedom was amazing. The air smelled more of jet fuel than salt water, but it was fresher than the recycled stuff they'd been breathing. After collecting their luggage and rebooking their flights for later in the afternoon, they were left with a five-hour gap with nothing to do. It wasn't long enough to hit a tourist trap, nor short enough to hang in the airport concourse.

"We could see the ocean," Glinda suggested. She'd never been to Hawaii, and with her schedule, it would likely be a while before she got another chance to visit. "I was hoping to get to the Pearl Harbor memorial but there's no way we have time for that now."

Before she knew it, they were in a taxi and on their way to the nearest beach.

Glinda wasn't up to eating, so she nibbled at a pretzel while Mike loaded up at a food truck. In his ball cap and sunglasses, he was completely anonymous. She'd done her best, tying her hair in a ponytail and stuffing it under a hat, and adding her own sunglasses, but her bust still drew glances. With so much other skin on display, she hoped to pass as just another tourist.

"Should you be doing that?" he asked.

She tossed a piece of pretzel into the flock of half dozen pigeons who'd bravely walked up to the bench they were using as a table. "Do what?"

"Feed them like that."

She threw another piece. Two more birds hopped over and began to fight over it. "They're just birds."

The two pigeons who'd joined the party invited their friends over, and suddenly there were two dozen birds pecking at their feet. "Maybe we should move," she hedged. One hopped onto the bench between them and eyed Mike's hot dog. "Yep, we're done," she amended.

A second later, they were dive-bombed by a seagull who pulled the hotdog out of its bun and swooped off again. The army of pigeons surrounding them erupted in cacophony of pissed-off clucks, and the one on the bench called his buddies up to divide the remainder of the spoils.

"Run!" Mike jumped to his feet, pulling her along with him. The birds followed, taking to the air to flank them from above. "This is insane!"

Glinda eyed the leader of the flock and took aim with the remnants of her pretzel. She pulled back her arm and let fly.

She didn't get close. The pretzel bounced harmlessly off the sidewalk into the overgrown grass at the edge of the path.

Mike groaned, then pulled a bag of chips out of his jacket pocket. He ripped it open and spilled the chips on the sidewalk. The distraction worked; the birds attacked the chips while Mike pulled her to safety.

Glinda collapsed on the closest bench, giggling helplessly. "Just call me Tippi. Holy hell, what was that?"

"I hadn't heard anyone was remaking *The Birds*. Or that we were starring in it. Are you okay?" To add insult to injury, Mike's stomach roared at the loss of the potato chips.

"I'm fine, but we'd better get you fed before you attract more wildlife. You sound like a lion calling for his lost pride members. Besides, I want another pretzel."

"I though you weren't hungry."

"The fresh air and blast of adrenaline seem to have cleared up my nausea. All of a sudden, I'm ravenous," she admitted. Her stomach was still a little off, but it was nothing she couldn't handle.

A pigeon fluttered to a landing a few feet away. Glinda grabbed Mike's hand again. "Come on. I have a craving for fried chicken."

Chapter Six

The growling wasn't from the propeller engines. It was coming from Glinda's stomach. Mike looked at her white-knuckled grip on the armrests and sighed. The LA-to-Honolulu flight had been epically bad. He couldn't deny it. But didn't that mean they should catch a break for the second leg of their trip?

Lightning flashed around the plane, illuminating the gray clouds above them. The hop from Honolulu to the Big Island was barely long enough to get them in the air, but it was more than enough time to bounce them around like a rubber ball in a washing machine. Glinda was trying to stifle her dry heaves, since her fried chicken didn't last through take-off, but it was a wasted effort. In such close quarters, everyone knew who was hoarding the air-sickness bags.

He'd never flown with a woman as sensitive as Glinda, but she was still one of the best travelling companions he'd ever had. Despite all that had gone wrong—and it had all gone wrong, no doubt, from their delayed take-off to this latest disaster—she had done her best to keep a positive attitude.

"You're doing great, Glinda."

"Mm-hmm."

"We're in final approach."

"Mm-hmm.

"I've decided that we're even from you pushing me out of the path of that falling light on the set."

"Mm-what?"

"I saved your life back there. Taunting a pigeon with a pretzel. That's like waving a salmon in front of a grizzly bear."

"Exaggerating much?" Her big, green eyes were focused on his face, and her death-grip on his hand eased minutely. If he could keep Glinda engaged, her stomach might have a chance to settle.

"I don't think so. You were seconds from being swarmed. I saved your life. Those things were vicious. Television star Glinda Crawford pecked to death by pigeons. Film at eleven."

"Funny."

"I thought so."

The dark skies and faint evening light meant the runway snuck up on them. They bounced twice, tires squealing when they hit the asphalt. Then they rolled to a stop.

"I've never been so glad to get somewhere in my life," Glinda said. She kept hold of his hand for balance all the way down the narrow rolling staircase.

"*What do you mean*, you don't have our luggage? There were only eight people on the plane."

"I'm sorry. We had weight restrictions, and your suitcases had to be left behind. We'll get them to you as soon as we can," the woman behind the airline's check-in counter said.

Glinda cut him off. "I don't have the energy for this. When will we get our bags?"

"We'll try to get them to you tomorrow."

"No, you will get them to us tomorrow. In the meantime, the airline offers compensation for lost or missing luggage. We're going to need that, now."

"It's not really missing," the airline representative hedged.

"Two hundred dollars is barely enough to cover toothbrushes, PJ's, and a change of clothes. Voucher. Now." Even after being sick for hours, and having the rug pulled out from her again, Mike was impressed that Glinda still acted like a lady. A lady who was obviously working hard maintaining her cool while giving orders, but she was still quieter that he would have been if he were the one doing the talking. She wasn't causing a scene, but she was going to get her way. They all knew it.

The woman handed over the demanded compensation. "I'm sorry to tell you this, but most of the stores around here close at six. There's nowhere to shop at this hour."

Their luck didn't get any better once they arrived at their accommodations for the next week but he was too tired to care.

He didn't give too much thought to the trailers the production company provided. It was late and dark, and he needed clean and a good night's sleep. The small propane heater in the galley kitchen pumped out warmth without a problem, so he rinsed his shirt and shorts and hung them in the kitchen. The bedroom in the back had thick curtains, a queen-sized mattress, and fresh sheets. He'd save the rest of his exploring for another day.

When he awoke, he wasn't alone. A pair of beady black eyes stared at him from across the room. The bat in the corner yawned, stretching its wings to their full span. "You should know, I'm a Superman fan," Mike said. His clothes were finally dry; draping them over the propane grate had worked, but it had also cooked in the wrinkles. Since he had no other options, he grabbed them, and inched towards the door in his boxers.

Mike gave an undignified yelp and burst through the door. He stumbled to a stop in front of Glinda, who wore a matching pissed-off expression.

"What did you have?"

"Bat. You?"

"Gecko. Like this." She held her hands a yard apart. "It was in the shower, which didn't work. It got in through the broken window. I thought you took this job so you could wear pants?"

"Crap." He pulled on his shorts and fumbled at the fly. He'd worn less on set but that was on purpose. This was almost flashing her. "I guess I have to go back inside for my shoes."

"Probably. I do have some good news, though."

"You found an exterminator? And he does bats?"

"No. I found an ally. Erin Thorne is our hair person." *Olympus*'s premiere hairdresser. "Her boyfriend is here with her, and he has graciously agreed to run into town and pick up some essentials for us. I already gave him my list."

That was the last thing to go right for days.

MIKE CROUCHED UNDER THE TARP, holding his side down in a fruitless attempt to block the driving rain which had plagued the shoot since the first day. Beside him, Glinda struggled to keep her section from flapping in the wind howling down the gully. They were waiting, again, for the second unit director to return from wherever he'd disappeared to. Again.

"How are you doing?" she whispered, one hand covering the microphone clipped to the bra under her sodden shirt.

He suppressed the cough he felt building in his chest. Then he ignored the question so he wouldn't have to lie to her. Glinda didn't need the extra stress. "This is worse than yesterday. I dare you to find a bright side to this."

He moved closer, and wrapped his free arm around her waist, pulling her close so her back was snug against his chest. The move was partially to conserve body heat, but was mostly an act of comfort between two soldiers.

Because he knew, without a doubt, they were at war.

It wasn't with diseased pandas. It was with a rabid second unit director with dictatorial delusions of grandeur. Four days. It had only been four days. Mike had been on bad shoots before. He'd worked on toxic sets where the cast infighting infected the crew and made the situation intolerable for everybody working there.

This was different. This was one man with the power to bring down a movie, and for some reason, Ferris Lorde was doing his damnedest to do it. Lorde was on an ego trip and trying to break anyone who dared speak against him. The continuous shouts of "I am God on this set. Who are you to question me?" gave it away. The entire crew was on the verge of revolting. The day before, the best boy and the location assistant outright told Mike that he and Glinda were the only things holding the shoot together.

Lorde must have heard the same thing, because he doubled down on his behavior the next day, demanding Mike and Glinda stay alone in the gully between shoots for "continuity purposes."

Which was how they ended up sitting in a jungle, in the rain, with a piece of plastic protecting them from something that would have driven anyone sane indoors.

It was probably a gorgeous location when it was sunny and dry. Trees towered over the rough hiking path that cut through the state park. Mike identified at least a dozen different types of trees and ferns, but they were all the same shade of gray-green in the poor light. Even the chestnut-brown loam was washed out by the film of water that couldn't soak into the already saturated ground.

"You want a bright side? I'll give you three. One, we're one day closer to being finished this shoot," she whispered.

"That doesn't count. You said that yesterday."

"It was true then, and it's true today," she argued. "Two, the weather reports say this crap is supposed to end this afternoon, and we're supposed to have sunny skies for the next week."

A crack of thunder overhead made them both duck. Mike would believe it when he saw it. "I'll give you a maybe on that one. What's the third reason?"

She turned her head over one shoulder. Since they were under a tarp, she couldn't see behind her anyway. Then she shoulder-checked the other side. She leaned toward him and whispered conspirically, "The celery stalks at midnight."

"What?"

"I have the orange of my aunt in my handbag," she said it a surprisingly good French accent.

"Do you have a fever?" He was coming down with a cold, which was bad enough, but if Ferris had made Glinda sick, he'd make sure the man paid.

She laughed, and for a second the relentless pounding rain and gray skies faded away. "I got a coded dispatch to the allies through the resistance." She must have recognized the confusion on his face, because she continued. "I left messages with both Fiona and the SAG offices to send a representative to this location to report on union violations. They should be here tomorrow at the latest. Lorde may think otherwise, but his authority stops where the union rep and the lawyers say it does."

That was hardball. Nobody liked it when lawyers got involved. Things got messy and expensive, two things producers wanted to avoid at all costs. But Glinda was right to do it. They could have caused a scene and refused to come out of their broken-down trailers; nobody would blame them. Instead, she'd decided to play by the rules and let the hammer come down where it was supposed to. Any fallout would miss them both.

He just didn't know how she did it. Their remote location meant cell phone service was nonexistent, and Lorde kept them busy enough that driving to the closest town wasn't a viable option. Not to mention, Lorde held the keys to the vehicles on the site. "For security purposes," the director said.

"When did you call?" Mike asked.

"Last night, after we wrapped for the day. I took a four-mile run to that little town up the highway, where, by the way, my cell phone worked. Then a four-mile run back here, and caught a catnap before our call time. Fiona is not going to be happy."

Their agent was going to be less happy when she learned what Lorde had pulled that morning. "Okay, I admit it. You found a bright side."

"Eventually everybody learns, Mike. My name makes me sound like a pushover but I've had my whole life to learn how to stand up for myself."

The rain began to ease. Not enough to get rid of the tarp, but they could see the other side of the gully. Mike wanted her to keep talking. It distracted him from the chill that was settling into his bones. He remembered an interview somebody had done with her. "Didn't you change your name when you moved to L.A.?"

She shifted so she was closer to him. They both shook at the force of the shiver running through her. "Yes. Why?"

"You said people have been judging you your whole life because of your name. But you've only been Glinda for a few years."

Her eyes widened in understanding. "Oh, no, I have been Glinda my whole life. I changed my last name."

"Your last name? What was it before?"

"Crabbe. Extra B, E on the end. You would not believe how many "ew, Glinda has crabs" jokes I suffered through in high school. As soon as I could, I changed it to Crawford."

"You didn't have any problems with Glinda?"

"Of course, I had problems with Glinda. I'm named after a witch who *defines* " bubbly blonde." But I have a twin sister. If I changed my name, hers would just be weird."

"You have a twin?" A picture appeared in his mind that he had no right to imagine.

"Three guesses on her name. The first two don't count."

The only Glinda he knew was from *The Wizard of Oz*, which meant… Her parents didn't. "Dorothy?"

"Yep. The Crabbe girls. She's tall, dark haired, and gorgeous. I'm short, have what she calls golden ringlets, and a bust that makes me the epitome of a blonde joke. But I know how to handle the jokes. I can deal with name calling. What people fail to consider is that after a lifetime of it, there are no original jokes left. I'm a pro at stopping bullies in their tracks. One of the best ways to do that is to call in bigger bullies. Hence, Fiona, union reps, and lawyers. Little Ferris is one more safety violation from an official complaint to the DGA."

"I'll keep that in mind."

"You'd better. You don't want to end up like Ferris."

She made him laugh. "There's no need to get mean."

Chapter Seven

"It's unsafe, Ferris." She called the tiny tyrant 'Ferris', because he'd asked her to call him Mr. Lorde, which she would have done if he'd returned the courtesy. But he didn't, so she didn't. It was petty, but at this point, rudeness was one of the few weapons Glinda had left.

"Everything's fine. A seasoned film actress would know that, Glinda, and would trust her director. She wouldn't cause a scene and undermine him in front of the crew."

"I'm pretty sure the crew agrees with me on this point. Everything is not fine. The local crew says there have been two landslides half a mile from here. This creek bank is dangerous. It can't take any more water. Every time we scramble up, more mud and rock rains down on us. The rope ladder the guys laid out has been completely covered by mud. We physically cannot do what you want."

She wasn't whining. Or yelling. She was fighting to keep from crying because she was ninety percent sure she'd broken a finger on the last take. Lorde had told her to walk it off. When she'd lost her temper and cursed him out, it had stunned him into silence. For a minute.

It had been worth the lecture on professionalism.

"You can, and you will."

Mike straightened to address Ferris. At least, he tried to. They were ankle deep in muck, and the ground beneath that was slick. He ended up leaning on Glinda like a drunken sailor. "We're done, Ferris. Come on, Glinda, let's get out of this hell hole." He reached for the line an enterprising production assistant had thrown down to help them in and out of the gully.

The rope slithered over the edge of the overhang.

Lorde stood up, a knife in his hand. "Oops. It looks like I accidentally cut off your exit route. Since you're stuck down there, we might as well get one more take," he said with a smirk.

Mike tilted his head towards a boulder which was sticking out of the nearly vertical wall. It was the only solid thing they could use to make the climb to top of the escarpment. He looked at her, and she agreed to his silent question without a word spoken.

She led the way.

They headed upstream, doggedly trekking through the cold water which spilled over the top of their boots. Behind them, Lorde shouted instructions. When they refused to respond, it simply became shouting.

When Mike lost his balance, she thought he'd found some bad footing. Then the ground shifted under her feet too, and she realized the gully floor was moving.

"Go, go, go!" Mike had his hands under her arms and was half-carrying her in the other direction before he got the words out.

She saw the boulder shift as a hunk of earth fell near its base, exposing more rock. The gap was immediately filled with mud and debris running down the side of the cliff, which pulled away more clumps and stones. "It's going to fall!"

The rain stopped. And the wind. The entire world went silent for a moment. Glinda thought the growing roar was her blood pounding in her ears. She tried to run, but every step meant she had to dislodge her foot from the mud like a suction cup.

The boulder pulled away from the gully wall, and the mud slipped into the cracks it left, serving as further pressure to dislodge it. The large, oval rock balanced on its base for a moment and then crashed to the ground.

They'd made it twenty feet in the seconds since they'd noticed the danger. The boulder ate six of those feet. Glinda could practically reach out and touch the thing that tried to kill her.

The rushing in her ears got louder. Mike looked at her. "Do you hear that?" he asked. She hadn't had time to answer before his eyes got big. "Up. We need to get up!"

There was no place to go. She pointed at the exposed root from a moss covered koa tree. "Give me a boost!"

He weaved his fingers together and bent over. Glinda stepped into his hands and fought to keep her balance as he hoisted her three feet in the air. It was enough. The rough bark cut into her hands, but she kept climbing. She rolled onto the sodden leaves and twigs lining the forest floor and dropped her hands back over the edge.

She could see around the corner of the gully from her vantage point. What was coming took her breath away. "Take my hand!"

He leapt, his height working to his advantage. He grabbed the same root she had, and his other hand wrapped around her wrist. She didn't have the strength to heave him to safety. All she could do was be an anchor for him to use. And she could hold on.

The water rushing down the gully hit like a wall. Mike was horizontal before she could blink, his legs and body lifted by the force of the current. She wrapped her legs around the trunk of the tree so she could hold onto his arm with both hands.

Suddenly, ice-cold fingers grabbed her at her elbow, and moved up to her underarm. She shifted her shoulder to give him a better handhold. Inch by inch, he pulled himself up, using her like a human ladder until he, too, lay on the embankment. She was still holding onto his hand.

Simply breathing took all her strength. Her arms were rubber. Her legs were too, but both burned as the new cuts and scrapes were exposed to the air.

"Are you okay?" Mike rasped.

"Dandy. You?"

"I think counts as my cardio for the week."

"We got the shot but, Glinda, you referred to him as Mike rather than Montgomery. I expect better," Lorde said.

She hadn't heard the director approach. Glinda rolled to her knees, and pushed herself up one arm at a time. Mike did the same, and they helped each other to their feet. She took a moment to find her balance. Then, holding onto to Mike's arm as support, she reared back and delivered a bootless kick between Lorde's legs, lifting him off the ground.

Chapter Eight

Mike didn't wait for an ambulance. A local production assistant loaded him and Glinda into the back of a minivan and drove them straight to Hilo, delivering them to the Emergency Room door. They weren't the only flash flood victims, but they weren't among the more seriously injured either, so they claimed a couple chairs in the waiting room. Ferris Lorde arrived by ambulance an hour later and was taken right into surgery.

Like the other patients-in-waiting, Glinda watched him be taken away, wide-eyed and full of curiosity. Butter wouldn't have melted in her mouth. "Gee, that looks serious," was all she said. Mike bit the inside of his cheek to keep himself from laughing.

Mike's check-up was brief. The ER doctors released him with bruised ribs, bandaged scratches, and a warning to see his own doctor if his cough got any worse. He was back in the waiting area, wondering what was going on with Glinda, when Fiona burst into the hospital.

"Where is that miserable motherfucker?" was her greeting.

"Surgery, I think."

"Where's my girl?"

"In one of the cubicles with a doctor. She's been a while." He was beginning to worry. He was one-ninety. Glinda had held him as dead weight while he used her as a climbing structure. She could have torn muscles and dislocated joints trying to save his life. When they'd loaded her into the wheelchair to take her to the examination room, she moved like she'd been hit by a truck.

"I can't believe he cut your safety line."

"How could you possibly know that? How are you even here?"

"You made friends on the crew. Lorde didn't. One of them filed a complaint with their union rep two days ago. There was a safety officer on set this morning. He was in the background, but he was recording everything. I got caught at the airport after they lost my luggage, so I missed it. We must have crossed paths on the highway. By the time I got to the shooting location, you two were already on the way here."

"That explains the rep being on site, but Glinda says she only called you last night."

"I was already on my way. I have friends too."

That was when an orderly wheeled Glinda back into the waiting room. Her middle finger was in a metal splint. The others were curled into a loose fist, which she held protectively against her chest. Her opposite foot was wrapped in a tensor bandage. Her face twisted into a grimace as she scooted to the edge of the wheelchair. "Can we go home now?" she asked tiredly.

"I THINK THAT'S A WRAP."

Mike rolled his eyes. "Are you still trying to come up with the perfect quip for after you nailed Lorde in the balls? It was two days ago, Glinda. It's too late. Let it go." He caught himself reaching under his arm to rub the healing scratches along his ribs. It was good advice; he should take it himself.

Unfortunately, everything reminded him of that afternoon. The red welts resembling claw marks on his chest itched incessantly. The softball-sized bruise on his calf was still tender, though the coloring had faded into his normal skin-tone.

Glinda was in worse shape. As pale as she was, every bruise stood out like a purple polka-dot on her skin. She seemed to be ignoring them. Her hair was in pigtails, bright pink elastics peeking out between the curls that sat on her shoulders. Even her make-up was relaxed. Their meeting was in her hotel suite, and since Fiona was the third and final person attending, Glinda told them she wasn't dressing up.

Their agent was coming to them for several reasons, the least of which was that, with their second unit director up on charges and Lorde's union throwing a fit about their request to have his credentials revoked, *The Bamboo Mountain* was on hold while they recovered. Not only were they both beat to hell, Mike had developed a cough from being out in the rain for so long. The doctors were keeping a close eye on him to ensure it didn't turn into pneumonia.

It was a good time to have a strategy meeting about their next step.

"Cut this?" Glinda suggested. "Come on, Mike, help me out. When I'm writing my memoirs, I want people to remember me for more than simply saying, 'Ouch' when I kicked that asshole."

"Glinda, you twisted your ankle nailing him in the balls so hard you ruptured one of his testicles." He flinched just saying the words. "Trust me, that's more than memorable enough."

He helped himself to another orange juice from her mini-fridge, bringing another back for her.

"Did you talk to your folks?" she asked.

"Yes. My dad freaked when he heard the news report, so our video chat went a long way to making him feel better. He gave me grief for not having the sense to come in out of the rain." His father had also asked some pointed questions about the woman Mike had been clenching so tightly.

Mike couldn't blame him. He'd seen the footage. To a casual observer, or someone who was willing to ignore the context of the situation, the way he and Glinda patted each other and refused to let go gave their actions implications that simply hadn't been there.

The truth was that he and Glinda were good friends who had both been almost scared to death. Literally. Even if they never worked together again and lost all contact, they'd still be friends. But Mike couldn't see that happening. Not now. So, friends they would be, united in adversity and determined to help each other with whatever hurdles came next. With *The Bamboo Mountain*'s horrific start, he couldn't help but anticipate more.

Sure enough, the next one arrived with Fiona, who was working on an extra-large coffee. She dropped her phone on the glass-topped coffee table and made herself comfortable on the second sofa in the suite's living area. Glinda's entire suite was decorated in various shades of beige, which blended into the formless pastel paintings on the way. Mike thought the Honolulu hotel might have done it on purpose to drive guests into the vividly colored gardens and pool area outside. His eyes swept over the balcony, and he thought about moving their meeting out there. He could carry Glinda if he had to.

"Lucie is absolutely devastated about what happened. She swears she vetted Lorde fully, but my contacts say this isn't the first time he's run rampant on a set. Lucie has hired a new second unit director, who will be more than happy to wait until you're fully recovered to resume filming in Los Angeles. She's cutting the rest of the location shoots." Fiona drained the rest of her coffee. "Damn, you two had me worried when I got your message," she added.

Fiona had taken one look at their trailers and resettled them into the closest hotel she could find until they could return to Oahu. Now they were about to discover the future of their movie careers.

Glinda shifted in her easy chair, her smile never wavering, but a thick wrinkle appeared on her forehead. "Take a pain pill, Glinda. It'll help you relax and will help your muscles heal," he said.

"Bossy." But she listened to him. "Put your foot up. Elevating it will help with the edema on your calf."

He did. "Where do we stand?" he demanded of Fiona. "Do they really want to move forward in Los Angeles? We didn't get half of what she wanted in Hawaii. There are whole sequences we didn't get to."

Ferris Lorde had hours of footage of them tromping through the jungle in different costumes. In one set they were looking for a diseased panda, and in another they were searching for the source of the infection threatening the panda population. They hadn't done any of the scenes releasing the pandas back into the wild, or chasing poachers away from the habitat, or the funeral pyre.

Fiona hefted a mint green purse into her lap and withdrew two thin envelopes. "They've decided to do a rewrite. Everything can be shot back home."

"Are we talking about a few pages?" he asked. Getting an entirely new script after shooting had begun was never a good thing. It often indicated the movie was unsound, which led to speculation that the entire project would be unsalvageable. Most films couldn't recover from that kind of bad publicity.

"No."

"How much is being rewritten?"

She gestured at the envelope.

He removed the single page. The first change was to the title. "*Extinction Level Event*? What happened to *The Bamboo Mountain*? It doesn't sound like a drama anymore."

Fiona flinched. "It's not. They're changing direction."

"To?"

"Action-adventure-land."

"That can't be good," his co-star said. He and Glinda were on the same page.

"It's not that bad," Fiona countered. It was not a glowing recommendation. "It's a decent action flick from the notes I've received. You'll have fun doing it."

"We signed up for a drama."

"But you did sign the contract," Fiona reminded him.

Which was the risk actors took when they agreed to make a movie. "When are we going to see the new draft?"

"Next week. Go home. Recover. You'll get the scripts as soon as they're ready. You will be back to work before you know it, so rest up now."

Chapter Nine

Glinda paced in the green room, waiting for the production assistant to arrive and escort them to the set of Johnny Chung's *After Dark*. Martine Peeples, *Olympus*'s PR boss, was pimping the premiere of the show's fourth season, but Glinda was certain the host had other topics he wanted to discuss. Ferris Lorde's fall from grace had everybody talking. With the footage a P.A. had shot on his phone of her and Mike getting caught in the flash flood, they were in high demand on the talk show circuit.

"Should you be walking that much? Maybe you should sit down. I think you're starting to limp. Is your foot still sore?" Mike asked. He looked calm and collected in his sports coat and slacks, and none the worse for wear. She could hardly wait for her injuries to fade so people would stop asking about them.

"I can't sit down. If I sit down, I'm going to fiddle with my finger brace, and it took me forever to arrange it so it wasn't sticking straight up," Glinda said. She'd given the bird to everybody for four days before she figured out how to play with the angles.

They waited in the wings behind the maroon curtain while Johnny Chung finished with his guests from *America's Best Trained Pets*: a pair of dancing parakeets who liked disco, and a poodle named Polk who could both snarl and smile on command. Once the set was clear, he introduced them. "I know you're here to talk about the *Olympus* season premiere, but you're in the news for other reasons right now. Let's start with the video from Hawaii. It's unbelievable," the host said.

Glinda had seen it before, but she still flinched when she saw a log brush past Mike in the turbulent water. "You're lucky that didn't knock you loose."

"I knew you weren't going to let me go."

Johnny turned to them both after Mike pulled himself to safe ground. "That was absolutely thrilling. Some people are claiming it's a little too convenient that the cameras were rolling during your miraculous escape. What do you say to their accusations that it was a publicity stunt?"

Mike rolled his eyes. "You're right. It was totally staged. We got thousands of people to report flash flooding across the island, injure themselves, and go to the hospital to add authenticity. You caught us."

While Mike was spouting some very mild sarcasm, she was working on her brace. "I faked breaking my finger too. Want to see?" She held up her hand; her middle finger was twice as wide and a good inch taller than the others.

Johnny hissed in sympathy as he took her hand and examined it up close. "It's purple. Not faked," he told the audience. "Does it hurt?" he asked as he poked the tiny bit of visible, bruised skin.

"Ow! Yes, it hurts," She yanked her hand away and turned the brace back into a less offensive position.

They finished their segment, talked up a storm about *Olympus*'s upcoming season, and said their good-byes as the camera rolled. As they crossed the raised platform holding the host's desk and guest chairs, Glinda hesitated for a second. It wasn't a sound, not quite. The low thrum and the following high-pitched twang stood the hairs on the back of her neck up straight.

The next thing she knew, Mike wrapped his arm around her waist and she flew backwards, getting a hard introduction to the concrete stage. She was sure she screamed, but she couldn't hear it over the thundering crash of cracking wood and roar of crumpling metal.

"What is going on?" Glinda asked when the noise stopped. She couldn't see anything. There was a sliver of light to one side, but she couldn't see her hand in front of her face. Her nose tickled too; the air she couldn't see was choked with dust. Mike's body covered hers completely. He wasn't crushing her; they were just experiencing more body contact that most couples had during sex. Much more.

"I'm not sure. It didn't feel like an earthquake," Mike whispered in her ear.

"Can you shift over a little? You're squishing me."

"No. Something is laying on me."

"Are you two okay?" Johnny Chung's voice sounded very far away.

"Did you get the license plate of that truck?" Glinda shouted back.

"Since you're joking, I'll assume you're fine. I have no idea how, but the curtain mechanism failed, and it brought down a piece of my set wall. We're working on removing it. Stay there."

"Funny."

She heard more shouts and the sound of wood scraping against plaster.

"I'm blaming you for this," Mike said.

"For the curtain mechanism failing or for the wall falling on us?"

"Both."

"How is this my fault?"

"Nothing like this ever happens to me when you're not around. You are bad luck, Crawford."

"I'm bad luck? Do you think I normally walk around leaving destruction and natural disasters in my wake? No, that only happens when I'm saving your butt. I had an incident-free record before I started working with you. Now I'm lucky if I go a week without having to set the "days without a workplace accident" sign back to zero."

"Um, guys? Your microphones are still on," Johnny yelled.

"It's true," Glinda insisted.

"Tell us more about the falling light on set. Was that on the *Olympus* set?"

"Don't you have to evacuate the audience to safety or something?" Mike asked.

"Nope, everybody out here is fine. When was this?"

"Don't mind him, Johnny. It was on one of the last episodes we filmed last season. He's just upset I saved his life. Again."

"How's that?"

"It's complicated. You had to be there."

"Is there any footage?"

The air seemed thicker. The dust was settling, and now she was catching hints of Mike's cologne. She was getting warmer too, and only part of that was because she was squeezed into a tight space. One of Mike's knees was between hers, and his thigh was pressing at the junction of her legs. It was very hard not to squirm. "It might be on the DVD extras. I was amazing, by the way," she bragged.

"She hits like a linebacker. An itty-bitty linebacker, Johnny. Great form, but the only reason she took me down was because she hit me from behind when I wasn't expecting it," Mike said.

"Excuses, excuses. It was more like, 'Timber!'" She drew out the word. "And then a thud." That got the shaken-up audience laughing. While Mike protested her version of events, and kept up the banter with Johnny, she tried to wiggle her hands free to press against the wall trapping him. All she'd managed to do was feel up Mike's chest. She wasn't complaining, but he'd given her a gentle pinch to tell her to stop, so she had.

"Mike, it does sound like Glinda saved your life on the *Olympus* set," Johnny said.

"I did," she agreed.

"I saved yours in Hawaii during the pigeon incident," Mike argued.

"Oh, this we've got to hear. Pigeon incident?"

"In Hawaii, before the flash flood, there was this gang of attack pigeons," Mike began.

"Really, attack pigeons? You're going with that?"

"Who's telling this story, Glinda? Me, the hero. Picture it, Johnny. Hawaii, about a week ago. There I was, minding my own business, when I see this flock of attack pigeons heading toward me. A hundred of them, maybe more. Then they veered off, having caught sight of the pretzel Glinda was eating. She was completely oblivious to the deadly threat. I had to run into a swarm of them with nothing more to defend us than my quick wits and a bag of salt and vinegar chips. A small bag," he emphasized. "I used my chips as a diversion, dove into the killer flock, and pulled Glinda clear in the nick of time. Sadly, both the pretzel and the chips were sacrificed, but I saved us. That's exactly how it happened."

"Oh my God!" She was pleased her put-upon voice had just the right amount of amusement to it. "Whatever, Mike. I'm sure it happened just like that. I have video of the flash flood. As for the pigeon thing, pics or it didn't happen, buddy."

"Video is for amateurs. I saved your life tonight by not letting you get turned into a pancake in front of a live studio audience. I win."

"It's sounds like you two are tied," Johnny interrupted. "This has been fun, but I need you to prepare. We're going to try lifting the wall now."

She and Mike fell silent. He wiggled, trying to cover as much of her body as possible in case the lift went wrong. She appreciated it, but the rubbing and the grinding did nothing for the heat she was generating. Glinda wrapped her hands around the back of his head and his neck, trying to protect the vulnerable areas.

The set wall went straight up about a foot and began to slide sideways. She should have thought of that. For some reason, she was expecting them to stand it back on end. When the lead grip shouted "Clear", she carefully let Mike go.

Mike slowly sat up. After she nodded at him, he helped her up as well.

The set was a wreck. The backdrop—a shimmering scene of the ocean by moonlight—was split down the middle. The coffee table beside the guests' sofa was flattened, since it took the brunt of the fall, the four legs sticking out like a cartoon animal who'd been dropped by an anvil. If Mike hadn't taken her down where and how he did, that could have been her.

The audience burst into applause as they slowly climbed to their feet. She curtsied, and Mike bowed slightly. Then they carefully picked their way through the wreckage as they left the stage.

"I need aspirin," he said once they'd been freed from their mics.

"I have some in my purse."

"I need a whole bottle."

"Coincidentally, that's what I have. Be nice or I won't share." But she would. His back was probably one massive bruise because of her. He was her guardian angel. The least she could do was fork over some painkillers.

"I'm starting to think we shouldn't work together. For our own health."

She wanted to shake her head, but the jostling would only exacerbate her headache. "You're looking at this all wrong. If both of us hadn't been in those places, we wouldn't have made it. We need to stick together," she argued.

"You may have a point. I need to survive this movie so I can start my retirement."

"Aren't you a little young to be considering that?"

"I've been acting for thirty-some years, Glinda. That's retirement age."

"Are you serious?" He sounded serious. She took a critical look at him while he gathered his jacket. He looked fine, as in *fine*. Mike treated his body like a temple and it showed. He no longer had the college-boy softness to his face that most men had in their twenties, but the stronger version of his chin and cheekbones were flawless. He could work for another twenty years without going under the knife for maintenance if he wanted to.

"Fiona got me a two-year contract with *Olympus*, and we just finished the first. This movie was an unexpected opportunity I couldn't turn down, but I'm not actively looking anymore. She's looking to move me into more spokesman roles."

"But you love acting!"

He held the car door for her. "I'm not quitting tomorrow. But I've done a lot, Glinda. There's not much left for me to try."

Just because he was right didn't mean it didn't suck for her. She liked working with him. "I'd miss you."

"I promise to make sure you have another private bodyguard if I'm not around."

It was better than nothing.

Chapter Ten

Guardian Angel.

It was a hell of a headline. It was a hell of a photograph. He was staring down at Glinda with a possessive, protective look as he lifted himself off her; she had her hands wrapped around his neck gazing back up at him like a damsel after her knight had slain his dragon. Or so the article implied. Of course they were looking at each other. They were face-to-face when they hit the floor. It's not like they'd had a chance to move.

He knew because Glinda had tried. First, she'd shimmied her hips beneath him as she tried to find a position where he wasn't crushing her. He was a grown man; he didn't pop wood at everything. But it had been a difficult task to stay on track and make his body respond. Then she'd attempted to give herself some leverage and ended up running her hands all over his body. That hadn't helped either.

The caption on the photo stated Glinda was gazing at her hero, but it wasn't hero-worship on Glinda's face. She'd been concerned. Professionally concerned, because if he went down, filming would be delayed for another week, and they couldn't afford any more delays. That was all.

Mike wished the studio would push their start date. He hadn't needed to be checked out. He had a couple bruises, but it was nothing serious. Glinda was the one who'd hit the floor hard. He'd tried to take the brunt of the fall but everything had happened so fast.

His cell phone rang right on schedule. He glanced at the call display but he already knew who'd be calling thirty seconds after the morning news entertainment section. "Hi, Dad. I'm fine. Glinda is fine. It was an accident and we're all fine."

"Are you going to tell me again how that Glinda girl is just a friend? I've got a bad knee. I don't think I could stand you pulling my leg any harder."

"Dad!"

"I'm looking a picture of the two of you right now. There's more than co-workers going on," his dad insisted.

"Dad, Chuck Wilson looked at you the same way after you pulled him out of the Watkins Factory fire, and I'm pretty sure you two weren't getting horizontal." Mike had been used to his dad being at risk every time he left the house to go to the fire hall. But that particular fire had been memorable. What should have been a simple two-alarm dumpster fire had jumped to a five-alarm blaze when oil drums on the other side of the building wall began to go up. It was the closest Mike had ever come to losing his dad.

"That was different. That was life or death."

"This was pretty close."

His father huffed into the phone, and Mike knew he'd made his point. "If things do develop, I'd prefer to hear about it in person and not on the news, Mike."

"Of course, Dad. If I meet the one, you'll meet her soon after. I promise. But Glinda and I are friends. Nothing is going to happen. But I am going to look after her, because she is a walking disaster. I have no idea how long she's survived this long."

"You do that. She's a funny girl. Take care, son."

His phone rang again, and it was another call he couldn't ignore. "Hi, Fiona. I'm fine. Glinda is fine. It was an accident, and we're all fine." His coffee was ready just in time. His formidable agent was not going to be pleased at this latest development. He tossed the pod and reset the single-serve machine for the next morning.

"You didn't think to call me?"

He had thought of it, but there was nothing Fiona could do about it after the fact. It was scary but nobody got hurt. "I think we'll get good ratings when that show airs."

"That isn't what I meant, Mike."

"Are you pissed about the liability paperwork? Because you have assistants for that."

"It's not about that."

Which meant it was mostly about the paperwork. Mike didn't blame her; he didn't like shuffling paper either. "We're okay, Fiona. I should go. Today's our first meeting with the new second unit director and I don't want to be late. Is there anything else I can do for you?"

"Robert Roth. I don't know where Lucie keeps finding these guys, but I am not amused. Let me know if you have any problems beyond the usual."

"Like him cutting security lines?"

"Or weenie wagging."

"Jesus, are you serious?" Where was Lucie Caruso finding these clowns?

"I'm not saying he dropped trou on a set a couple years ago "to make the actress more comfortable" during a nude scene. I'm just saying that should his pants fall down, I want to know about it. I hear he prefers blondes."

He dumped his coffee down the drain, having lost all appetite for it. "I'll keep that in mind. Bye, Fiona."

Chapter Eleven

Glinda woke to a brand-new set of aches and pains. Her new phone had a cracked screen, but she was still able to make a note to send flowers to her stunt double as a belated and advanced thank you for the beatings she'd received and was sure to take again. Her driver got her home and helped her to the front door. She took off her makeup and fell into bed. It was a good thing she'd set the alarm before she'd left for Johnny's show, because she slept right through the night.

It was the second night in a row she'd done that; there was nothing like sleeping in her own bed, no matter how nice a hotel was. She'd dreamed of Mike again, which was no surprise. In Hawaii, she'd dreamed he was an Indiana Jones-type adventurer, and they were on the run from a river that changed directions because of a Nazi-designed remote control. Last night they'd been stranded on a deserted island. She woke after he'd built a lean-to and a fire, and they were having a clam bake. She didn't know what significance the clams had, but the rest was obvious enough. She had a crush on her co-star.

She needed to kill it immediately.

It wasn't her fault. *Relationships based on intense experiences never work.* She heard that in a movie once, and she'd proven it true. Of course she might develop feelings for a big, strong, handsome man who had saved her life. She wasn't made of stone. She preferred not to date where she worked, but it wasn't an iron-clad rule. Mostly it was a holdover from her younger days. Mike was mature enough that they'd be able to avoid most of the star-dating-star drama that came from the flavor-of-the-weeks when they lived their relationships in the spotlight. The problem was he wasn't interested in her romantically, and she had to respect that if she was going to work closely with him for the next couple months.

Sometimes being an adult really sucked. Glinda gave her feelings a stern talking to and shoved them down deep. She had work to do.

Rush hour traffic was its normal, abysmal crawl, but she had left early enough to be on time. She tossed her empty coffee cup into the recycle bin outside the meeting room and entered the table read with a smile on her lips.

The first person she saw was her new second unit director. Robert Roth was a fifty-year-old former wunderkind director. He was falling behind these days to second unit jobs as new up-and-comers edged him out of the slots he used to hold so easily. Being called in as a replacement must have been a blow, and he'd evidently decided to pass on the insult.

"Glinda, I'm glad you could join us." His face looked venomous, and she had no idea why. "Perhaps you can be on time tomorrow." She hadn't worked with

Roth before, but ten seconds in, he was bringing to life every comment she'd heard about him. With both Fiona's warnings and Dory's reminder to stand up for herself fresh in her mind, Glinda decided to make it known exactly where she stood.

She glanced at the clock on the wall. "I'm ten minutes early."

"If you're not fifteen minutes early, you're late. Keep that in mind, please, out of respect for the rest of us."

She sat down and noticed Mike's chair beside her was still empty. Lucky guy. This was going to be just as much fun as their time with Lorde. She could tell.

Her co-star entered five minutes later, trailed by an administrative assistant she recognized from the studio's publicity department. Mike scrawled his signature, returned her clipboard, and took it back when she flipped to another page and indicated for him to sign again.

"Mike, pleased to meet you. Robert Roth," Roth gushed. He stuck out his hand and offered all kinds of pleasantries he hadn't bestowed on her. And he didn't say one word about Mike being fifteen minutes early.

She knew she wasn't hiding her shock. Mike frowned at her upset look. "I'll tell you later," she mouthed. He took his seat.

All the chairs were filled, but Roth waited until the minute hand hit the twelve before he started. "I'm here to clean up Ferris Lorde's mess. Rest assured, we will not be repeating that experience. Some of you worked together in Hawaii. I've brought in my own people to fill the more immediate gaps. I'll be bringing in others later. Let's do some introductions."

Glinda was pleased to see Matti West, a former gymnast and circus acrobat who doubled for her and a couple other actresses on *Olympus*. The short blonde from South Carolina was a close physical match, but Glinda had eight years on her. If Matti wanted to take the bumps and falls for her, she was welcome to it.

She watched Mike greet George Truman like a long-lost friend. The stunt man was as built as Mike; they were both sleek and tall, with muscles that came from activity rather than straight-up body building. George had a tattoo on his biceps peeking out from under his shirt sleeve, the thick black lines standing out on his dark skin. He'd have to cover them with make-up or wear long-sleeved clothes when he was working, since Mike was body-art free. Unless Mike had something on a butt-cheek. She'd seen the rest of him when he'd made his mad escape from his bat-trailer.

"Glinda, is there a problem? You're smiling."

"Smiling is a problem?" Roth was pulling all the classic dominance displays. He was technically in charge of the shoot, which meant he was owed a modicum of her respect. She should set an example for the rest of the cast and crew. However, she was not required to let him treat her like a doormat.

"It's not appropriate."

"I'm pleased to meet my new co-workers, one of whom is a friend of Mike's. I'm not going to frown at him. I'm not an asshole."

"I'm the director."

There was so much she could say to that, but she held her tongue and went with, "What does that have to do with me smiling during a meeting?" It was one of the scripts she'd learned in therapy to put bullies on the defensive. When Roth began to turn red, she realized all over again how effective it was.

He continued going around the table. She and Mike both held up proceedings when he got to his two safety officers. She wanted to be on very good terms with them. Roth broke up her conversation, insisting they had more important items on the agenda, but let Mike continue to chat while he lectured her on respecting people's time.

By the time they got to the script review, Glinda was ready to call it a day. "Let's look at the script. I've made numerous changes, and I want us all to be on the same page."

She could have nit-picked. They weren't *his* changes, not with the script only a week old. But she was sure they were coming. Roth was the sort to want to ensure his grimy little fingerprints were all over the finished project. By the time they were done, she'd bet money he'd be insisting on a screenwriting credit. But she let the misstatement go; they had enough to cover without her starting an argument she couldn't win.

Barely anything of the old script remained: her character, Mike's character, and some infected pandas. The rest was new. In the shift from drama to action-adventure, Dr. Hanzel's selfless veterinary virology work had become a mystery looking at a failed biological attack that had spread like wildfire through certain branches of the animal kingdom instead. Jane Mackenzie was still an Army officer, but now she was helping Dr. Hanzel track down a terrorist cell.

There were a couple of jungle scenes, although they had nothing to do with pandas and everything to do with escaping eco-terrorists. It was possible their death-defying exploits would stay in the movie.

Ferris Lorde was upfront about trying to kill them. Robert Roth was going for a death by a thousand cuts form of homicide.

So far that morning, he'd attempted to gaslight her about being late, and moved straight to mansplaining her profession to her in front of the cast and crew she was supposed to work with. She waited for him to take a breath, which took longer than it should because the man loved the sound of his own voice and had amazing breath control. "Robert, before you continue, can we just stipulate that, in the interest of being respectful to everyone's time, if somebody in the room is unfamiliar with an industry term, they can simply ask, rather than you explaining to me what a transport captain does or what a greensperson is?"

"I'm making sure everyone knows what's going on, Glinda."

"Actually, Robert, you've directed every single one of those comments to me, specifically. I know this because you just said, 'Glinda, the greensperson is going to be responsible for all the plants on the set to maintain the jungle atmosphere we need'." She could handle the insults; she wasn't a baby. But if she didn't call him on undermining her—a lead—in front of the rest of the cast and crew, she was never going to get the respect that she needed. That she'd earned.

"I didn't—"

"You did, Robert," Mike interrupted. "I think it's great you're willing to explain everything, but Glinda, and the rest of us, are seasoned professionals. It's not needed. You were right when you said we were behind the eight-ball when it came to scheduling. Let's save some time without cutting corners."

Roth turned interesting shades of colours, but he didn't refute Mike's statement. Which was also irritating. She knew Mike wasn't doing it on purpose. In fact, he was likely trying to support her. It was galling that she needed a man to make another man listen to her.

But it was nice to have the back-up. It would have been nicer if he'd stopped Robert's tirade before she had to. Glinda knew from Robert's glare that she hadn't made any friends with her comment. She'd likely be paying for it for the rest of the shoot, but it was a price she was willing to pay. She couldn't blame Mike for wanting to avoid the same fate.

By the time they were through the new script, Glinda was ready for a liquid lunch. But the fun wasn't over yet.

Roth dismissed them for an hour before they started blocking the first scenes to be shot on the soundstage. "Glinda, I made sure they'll have a salad waiting for you. We want to make sure you'll be able to fit your wardrobe, won't we?" The bastard smiled when he said it. Smiled right at her, turned on his heel, and strode off. Probably back to the eighth ring of hell where he came from.

The room emptied quickly after that, people shooting her looks of smugness or sympathy. Soon only she and Mike remained.

"Do you think it's too late to get Lorde back?" Mike asked.

Chapter Twelve

The crew had been close. The set was a decent replica of the state park near Hilo where they'd been shooting. There were more palms than koa trees, but they got the density of the vegetation right. The fake moss and peaty soil weren't authentic, but nobody would be filming close-ups of the ground. More importantly, there wasn't a stream threatening to turn into a river and wash them away. An enterprising gaffer had managed to run some of the electrical wires through the hollow tree trunks so they reappeared twenty feet up and disappeared into the green canopy. For the moment, to all appearances, he and Glinda were taking a friendly walk in the woods.

"Let's reset. Glinda, try not to miss your mark again." Robert Roth's voice echoed across the set. "This is what happens when you can't pick your own lead actress," he muttered, but he did it loud enough she could hear him. Every grip and production assistant in earshot winced. It had never been funny. Some of the crew had initially smirked at the lead actress being publically corrected by the second unit director, like being blonde meant she was too stupid to know how dumb she was being. That amusement had run out in a matter of days, when they realized Glinda was fine; the problems—all of them—stemmed from Roth. Unfortunately, nothing could stop his constant verbal assaults on Glinda.

In all his years of acting, Mike had never met anyone as skilled as Glinda in covering up her microphone so she wouldn't be overheard or recorded when she didn't want to be. "Do you want me to ask for a break?" he offered, knowing she'd be berated if she asked for one herself.

"I'm fine. Let's get this scene done. It's been a long day, partner."

She wasn't fine. She flinched every time she heard Roth's voice, although she did her best to hide it. Mike ran interference wherever he could, but it didn't seem like nearly enough. He didn't know what else he could to support her. He pulled his wire from the mic pack to guarantee them some privacy. "I'll bet I can find a bright side to this long day."

She cocked an eyebrow. "Do tell."

"We're one day closer to being finished this shoot."

"That doesn't count. You said that yesterday."

"It was true then, and it's true today," he teased.

"Five weeks to go." She smiled, but her eyes weren't in it.

Mike couldn't bear it. He gently pulled her until her forehead rested on his chest, then wrapped his arms around her. "Five more weeks. And most of that should be with Lucie Caruso. If we get through this sequence we'll be free and clear."

"Shouldn't she be here already? This is odd, right? Having a director not show up for their first movie? Second unit directors are fine, but she should have appeared for something instead of video meetings and emails."

"I'm sure there's a precedent. It'll be fine," he promised.

He felt Glinda inhale deeply, then slowly exhale. He bent and dropped a gentle kiss on the top of her head. "You've got this, Glinda."

"If Roth keeps this up, can I kick him in the balls?"

"Let's save that for a last resort?" Although he wouldn't blame her. Having seen her kick, and knowing her wardrobe called for steel-toed boots, he wouldn't try to stop her either.

They returned to their start positions, and Mike plugged his microphone back in. A couple yards back, out of frame, a gang of eco-terrorists waited to begin their chase. "Background. Action!"

Glinda pushed ahead. "Come on, doc. The Jeep's just ahead. Only a few more yards."

Mike hunched over as he stumbled behind her; the bad guys had cracked Dr. Hanzel's ribs while they were interrogating him for information. "How can you tell? It all looks the same."

The actors on their tails grunted and shouted directions to each other.

"I put a homing beacon on the vehicle. Look, there it is!" Glinda said as they entered what would pass for the edge of a clearing.

"Cut!"

They froze. Glinda looked down, and Mike saw her smirk before her head came up with a perfectly bland expression on it. He studied her feet, and saw the smallest hint of red electrical tape sticking out from beneath her boot. She'd nailed her mark.

When Roth approached, Glinda made a show of lifting her foot straight up and revealing the X beneath it. The director was riding her hard, but she hadn't caved yet. Little shows of rebellion were all she could afford without damaging the production schedule or the budget, but she took her victories where she could. Behind Roth, one of the grips gave them a thumbs-up.

"Glinda, go get your make-up fixed. You're a mess. Mike, I have a new scene for you. We're going to do it this afternoon."

That was so wrong. Dialogue changes, fine. Throwing a whole new scene at them? Mike accepted the pages without a word. He flipped through the stapled sheets. "Glinda and I both have no-nudity clauses."

"Which you can opt to waive. I want you to waive them," Roth said. "It's not a big deal."

"What's not a big deal?" Glinda stuck her freshly powdered nose between them. "Are those the new pages?"

Mike handed them over.

"Is that Jane's ass?" she asked. "Wow, they really shoehorned her naked behind onto the page, didn't they?" she said once she finished reading.

"My character is naked too," Mike protested.

"Your character doesn't rate a mention a close-up of his bare ass pressed against the driver's window. What is this?"

"A new scene I wrote," Roth said.

"Do you really think, plot-wise, that the hero and heroine should take a time-out for car sex when, in the previous scene, they are literally seconds ahead of the bad guys?" Her incredulous expression belied the serious tone of her question.

Roth turned his usual shade of red when dealing with Glinda. But she silenced him before he had a chance to speak. "We can do this setup, no problem. Who are our body doubles?"

"I want you to do it."

"No."

Then she stopped. Mike had been bracing for an argument. For tears. For yelling. Not a quiet, absolute refusal. Cute, bubbly Glinda had turned into an iron warrior in front of his eyes.

"But—"

"No. Did you want to run the chase scene again, or are we moving on?"

"Let's talk about this some more—"

"No."

"Mike, talk some sense into her."

"No." Twenty years in the business as an adult, and he had never shut a director down cold before. He was terrified. Whether *Extinction Level Event* was a disaster or not, the director ran the show, or in this case, the second unit director.

The silent standoff continued for another minute before Roth caved. He stomped off, muttering something along the lines of "We'll see about this." Mike could have compromised. He didn't have a problem with getting nearly naked on screen, but he wasn't going to leave Glinda hanging.

"Now what?"

"We toss it to Fiona and let her deal with it. That's why we pay her. I specifically told Lucie Caruso I was keeping my clothes on. I have no problem with them using body doubles, but my boobs and ass are not going on the big screen." She sounded so sure of herself, he was convinced. Until he felt her fingers shaking when she lay her hand on his forearm. "I assume we shouldn't leave in case he comes back. He didn't officially call it. Want to grab a bite?"

His stomach roiled at the thought. His brain overrode it with the reminder that they'd been working for eight hours already. Roth was unpredictable. They had no idea when they'd get another chance to eat. "Sure." He thought of something else. "You're making the call to Fiona."

Chapter Thirteen

Apparently, if Roth didn't get to see her breasts, he didn't want to see the rest of her. He dismissed everyone for the evening, which, thankfully, rolled them into a glorious day off in perfect Los Angeles weather. Glinda was going to climb into her queen-sized bed, pull her duvet over her head, and sleep till noon. Then, maybe a late brunch, followed by a quick trip to the grocery story to stock up on chocolate and other essentials, and an afternoon nap. She'd be booked the entire day.

"This is a nice surprise. What are you going to do tonight?" Mike asked. He stretched his arms, tapping the top of the doorframe on their way out of the soundstage. His shirt strained against the muscles in his chest.

Her words stuck in her throat. "I'm not sure. How about you?"

"I want to catch *Three Date Rule* while it's still in the theater. Have you seen it?"

Three Date Rule was a big deal to a lot of the *Olympus* cast. Chris Peck, who played Zeus on the show, was the leading man in the romantic comedy, and a new cast-mate, Caitlin Kelly, had a small part as well. Glinda had the best intentions to see it and show her support, but time had got away from her. "Not yet. I kept meaning to but…"

"Yeah." He hesitated. "Do you want to go with me?"

She wasn't tired anymore. It had been ages since she'd gone to a movie, and if she waited much longer, it would be gone.

"I'll spring for Junior Mints," he added, like he needed to sweeten the pot.

She snorted. "Popcorn or nothing." If she was going to be in an actual theater, she wanted the good stuff.

"Deal. I was planning to go to the Hollywood Octo-plex. Can I drive you there and bring you back for your car after the show?"

"Now?" She'd showered in her trailer. She washed off the sweat which had accumulated after hours of standing under spotlights all day, as well as removed her thick layer of make-up. She'd redone her hair and make-up and had changed into a perfectly acceptable casual outfit: jeans, a thick, leather belt, and a tan, scoop-neck shirt with beading around the neck. Her purse even matched the turquoise stones around the collar. But she wasn't dressed up to go out.

"You look great. You don't need to go home and change, do you?"

Not if her date was already telling her how good she looked. Glinda did want to swap out the runners she was wearing to drive. She knew she didn't have anything appropriate in her trailer. She remembered a pair of leather sandals in the trunk of her car. "Thank you. No, I need to swing by my car first, but I'm good to go."

Mike was also in jeans, but he was in a button-down shirt and good shoes. He'd also shaved off his five o'clock shadow. He was date ready.

"I like this. I'm not usually spontaneous," she said with more enthusiasm. This was good. Getting out and acting like regular people was exactly what she needed. It was what people did after a hellacious week at work. An early night to bed would have been good too, but she had the whole next day off. She could have groceries delivered.

Three Date Rule had been out for a month, so they had their choice of seats in the mostly deserted theater. Mike carried the drinks and she carried the tub of popcorn. She stuffed the Junior Mints into her purse because he had insisted he couldn't make it through a movie without them. At least he hadn't suggested sprinkling the candy on the popcorn. Caramel corn was one thing; melted chocolate and mint cream on the odd kernel was entirely different.

Nobody sat close enough to complain while they whispered back and forth during the previews, commenting on who they'd worked with, and who they wanted to. When the studio logo appeared on the screen, Mike slid deeper into his seat. "Not talking during the movie," he instructed.

"Of course not." She took a piece of popcorn and sucked on it very slowly. It was going to be difficult remembering not to give a running commentary. Dory hated when she did it too, but it had never stopped her. It was one of the reasons she seldom went to the theater any more. She could be quiet – if the movie was good enough to draw her in—but films that good were few and far between. She couldn't remember the last one that had wowed her into silence.

Three Date Rule was close.

Glinda jammed her fist against her mouth. Laughing was fine—it was a romantic-comedy—but she wanted to point at the screen and make jokes about Caitlin in a gingham dress leading a square dance in cowboy boots. It was the hair that sent her over the edge.

She felt an elbow bump against her ribs. "Are you okay?" Mike whispered.

"Pigtails!" Then she lost it again. She tried taking a sip of soda, but it went down the wrong way and she began to cough.

Mike patted her on her back. "Breathe, Glinda."

When she leaned back in her seat, she'd shifted so she was leaning against him slightly. He didn't seem to mind, so she didn't move. She told herself it was because of the warmth he gave off in a room she hadn't thought was cool before that moment.

When the credits rolled, the popcorn bucket was empty and Glinda was still starving. Her belly growled on their way out of the theater. She tried to ignore it, but Mike looked pointedly at her stomach. "Dinner?"

It roared again. She wanted to spend more time with him, but not if she had to guilt him into it. "I supposed it would be ridiculous to say I'm not hungry. I can pick something up on my way home."

"Not when T.J.'s is around the corner."

She'd heard of the award-winning steakhouse but she'd never eaten there. "We don't have reservations. It's nine-thirty. That's prime time."

"Don't say no for them. Let's see what they can do."

It turned out, T.J.'s could do a great deal for them, including finding a booth in the corner of a quieter than usual dining room. Their meal would take at least an hour, which meant she could have wine, something she refrained from when she was on location, and something she'd had to avoid while she'd been on painkillers from the accident. The by-the-glass menu had some interesting choices, so she went with a California red.

"Do you know much about wine?" Mike asked.

"Not really. There aren't a lot of wineries in Iowa. I prefer stuff that doesn't come from a box, but I have been known to slum when I'm desperate. How about you?"

He raised his beer bottle. "Dad wasn't much into wine."

"And your mom?"

"She died when I was a kid."

"I'm sorry. I—"

He patted her hand, and let his fingers cover hers for a moment. "It's okay, Glinda. It was a long time ago, and my dad is a great guy. He just isn't a wine guy."

"Do you have any brothers or sisters?"

"No, I was an only child. I have a couple cousins and I'm close to them, but mostly it was just me and my dad."

That didn't sound like much fun. She only had one sister but she had a dozen cousins. She was close to them all. When she spent holidays with her parents, their house always turned into a zoo.

"Do you want to try some of my wine?"

"No thanks. There's a reason I'm still a beer guy."

By the time their salads arrived, she'd spilled everything about her sister that he hadn't dug out when they were under their tarp in Hawaii. She'd even pulled out her phone and showed him a picture of her and Dory from the previous Christmas.

Mike blinked and then smiled. "Right. Fraternal twins." He smiled bigger. "Cute sweaters."

Glinda snatched her phone back. They were cute. "I don't know why all Christmas-themed sweaters are referred to as ugly Christmas sweaters."

"You have a one-eyed reindeer head on yours."

"I like it."

"He has a red pompom for a nose."

"It's not like it lights up or anything."

He set down his beer. "You say that like you are trying to differentiate it from another reindeer sweater you have which does have a nose that lights up."

She pressed her lips together. She wasn't getting into that discussion.

"I assume holidays were a big deal at your house."

"The biggest. You?"

"We celebrated them all. Not necessarily on the day, but we celebrated." Mike shrugged. "My dad was a firefighter. He was on duty for a lot of them but we made up for it when he was off. It's wasn't such a bad deal. I got to celebrate with whoever I was staying with while he was working, and then I got a second one for just the two of us. I was double-dipping into the presents long before Seinfeld made it cool."

"Two birthday cakes too?"

"Of course."

"That's alright then."

Maybe she wasn't as hungry as she thought. She ate half her salad, and she skipped the sourdough bread basket. She still only managed to eat half of her small steak. "I am stuffed." At this rate, she wouldn't have to go grocery shopping the next day at all. She'd still be full.

Mike wiped a piece of steak on his plate, picking up the last of the sour cream from his baked potato, and popped it in his mouth. "I think I have to agree with you. It was good though."

"Very good. Great recommendation."

He slipped the bill wallet beside his plate before Glinda even saw it arrive. "You can't."

"Of course, I can."

"You got the popcorn."

"And I'm getting the check too."

She wouldn't argue with a man who wanted to take her out to dinner. Especially such a delicious one. The walk back to his car was short, and the evening air had cooled to the point where she was glad she'd worn her jacket. It was delightfully brisk. Instead of her big meal lulling her into a stupor, she was full of energy.

"That's some pep in your step," Mike said.

"I know. I feel like I could keep on walking."

She didn't realize they weren't heading back to the studio parking lot until he turned onto Santa Monica Boulevard.

"Where are we going?"

Chapter Fourteen

He couldn't let a comment like that go. Not if it meant letting Glinda go home. She'd opened the door to keeping their date going, and he was going to barge right through. If she wanted to walk, he knew of a lot more romantic places than a restaurant parking lot.

Like the Third Street Promenade or the Santa Monica Pier. Girls loved the kitschy stuff, and a lot of Los Angelinos had never bothered to check it out. It was the perfect time of year to go; the evenings were cool but not the cold of winter in Southern California. He lifted his new jacket off the backseat of his silver convertible and slipped it on so they could drive with the windows down and the heater on.

Glinda had mentioned her twin sister before, but he had no idea she was so family-oriented. It was nice. Strange to his experience, but nice. A dozen cousins, which meant two dozen aunts and uncles, plus any kids the cousins had. He had no doubt she knew them all by name and, possibly, by birthday. She should have stock in a greeting card company because she was definitely the birthday card type.

Asking her to the movies had been testing the water. Asking her to dinner after was taking a step in the right direction. Now they were in dating territory. It was a good thing he'd spent two trans-Pacific flights deciding what he'd do with Glinda if he ever asked her out, because he'd had no time to prepare. At the moment, he was confidently optimistic.

He kept his hand on her back as he ushered her through the throngs of people going through the iconic pier entrance. When the crowds eased, she didn't move away. "It's too bad we can't go into the aquarium," she said.

"You've been here before?" So much for being original.

"Here. Randy's Donuts. Rodeo Drive. Hollywood Walk of Fame. If it's been featured in a film, I've been there. Those cousins I mentioned? Whenever they visit, they want to see everything. I can usually beg off Disneyland and Universal Studios, but as for the rest of it, I'm the chief chauffeur and tour guide."

The downside of having a thousand relatives. "You don't sound overly upset by it."

"It's family. What are you going to do? Besides, there are worse things in the world than visiting world-famous tourist traps."

"Like driving in Los Angeles?"

"I only do it on their first trip to California. After that they're on their own."

The aquarium was closed, but the arcade was open. Darts were not his friend. He dropped enough money to buy a dozen stuffed animals but eventually won a fuzzy tarantula on a stick. Glinda held it in front of them as they walked, letting it bounce and jiggle on its elastic loop. He'd offered to pick the stuffed green lizard for her, in memory of her trailer in Hilo, but she declined.

At first, he thought it was noise from the boardwalk, but the third time he heard it, he saw Glinda rubbing her stomach again. "Are you hungry?" Now that he thought about it, he could use a bite to eat.

"I can't be. We just finished supper."

Mike checked his watch. "Two hours ago."

"Really?" She smiled. He wasn't sure why, but something was going on in that head of hers. "You know, we didn't have dessert."

No, they hadn't. However, he could fix that horrible oversight. "There's a place on the Third Street Promenade. They have tortes that will knock your socks off." Ever since his father had discovered it, all his birthday cakes had to be ordered from the organic patisserie. And pies for Thanksgiving. And whatever other occasions his old man could wrangle a dessert out of.

They sat inside. Glinda wrapped her hands around her coffee mug, taking a break from the chocolate raspberry torte she'd drooled over in the display case. He'd gone for a piece of chocolate pecan pie, and made a mental note to never tell his father about it. If he did, he'd never get a piece if one came into the house.

"I'm disappointed, but not devastated," he admitted. "Honestly, *The Bamboo Mountain* was a beautiful script, and I would have been proud to be attached to it. But I've also wanted to break out of dramas and do an action picture. Despite its problems, *Extinction Level Event* has a pretty good story. I never would have had the chance to star in it if the contract hadn't already been signed. We can still have fun with it if—" they were in public "—things on the administrative side work themselves out."

They had to improve. Ferris had been a disaster, but he hadn't set out to ruin their shots. Mike had the feeling Roth was doing just that. He had no clue why the director would want the movie to flop, but he seemed to be doing his best to make sure it happened. Mike couldn't wait for Lucie Caruso to arrive so they could get things on track, and he could show off what he knew he could do.

Glinda nodded in agreement. "Jane Porter isn't some helpless bubblehead. It's really all I can ask for." Mike knew she was smarting over her character being reduced from an active, intelligent problem solver to hired muscle, but she said she was happy Jane was at least competent hired muscle. Maybe Lucie would be able to tweak some of the scenes to give Jane some deeper characterization. "And we get to meet our new co-stars next week."

He was ridiculously excited the pandas were coming. Not live ones on set, at least, not so he'd been told. However, he'd heard rumors they might be able to manage a live one for a scene or two. They'd been filming for a week and had done everything except a scene with the animals they were supposed to be saving. Mike expected a lot of green screen work with the pandas being digitally added, but Roth said there would be something for them to interact with.

He watched Glinda tap her fingers against the side of her mug, thumb to pinky and back to thumb. He didn't know how they'd ended up taking about work again, but he didn't want her to be bored. "Are you okay?"

"Mmm. Fine." The tempo increased. "Why? Are you okay?"

He stared pointedly at her hand. He didn't expect the blush. "Oh. Nervous habit. I'm not supposed to have coffee at night. Like ever. Unless we're doing night shoots. Because I'm really caffeine-sensitive."

"Then why did you order coffee?"

"Because I didn't want our date to end yet," she replied.

"You didn't think to order decaf?"

"I was too excited about the torte. You were right. It's to die for."

He'd take a back-handed compliment from a hyper Glinda anytime. She didn't even get offended when he laughed. "Do you want to go for a drive?"

"Where?"

"Nowhere. Just drive." It was a clear night; it was late enough the streets would be empty. There wouldn't be a better time to drive for the sake of driving than the present.

He turned north onto the Pacific Coast Highway. The full moon over the water lit the way for them. As the city thinned into suburbs and more empty spaces than peopled ones, the mood in the car got quieter. He kept his hand on the clutch, more out of habit than necessity because of the curves on the road. Soon after they cleared the city limits, Glinda reached out and lay her hand on top of his.

She was wearing sparkly blue nail polish, something she must have put on after they'd finished shooting but before she'd left her trailer for the night. The logic escaped him; she'd only have to take it off in a couple days anyway. But in the meantime, it gave her fingers an ethereal glow in the starlight. "Okay?" she asked.

Yeah, he was okay. He brought her hand to his lips and pressed a gentle kiss onto the palm. When he had to downshift, she ensured their hands stayed together. Sometimes they talked. Sometimes they lapsed into a comfortable silence.

They made it all the way to Santa Barbara before they turned around. It was almost five in the morning when they had to stop for gas. They pulled into a gas station, refueled on vending machine soda and chips, and were halfway home. "It's too late to quit now. Sunrise will be in an hour. I can't let a dinner date go home hungry. Can I buy you breakfast?"

"How about I buy you breakfast?"

"Ladies don't pay."

"You're about seventy years out of time, Mr. Mosley. If you pay, I'm picking up the check on our next date. Which, going by how long this one lasted, could go for days."

"Yes on the next date part, please. Good luck with the check." It wasn't that he didn't think she could afford it; she simply shouldn't have to worry about stuff like that. He was more than capable of taking care of things. Taking care of her.

"We'll see."

There was the Glinda he was becoming accustomed to. The one who didn't back down from a fight. It was funny; he'd always assumed she was easy-going, almost to the point of being a pushover. Give-along, get along. She rarely argued with directors, and only corrected writers when they made glaring continuity errors with Aphrodite's history. For the most part, she kept her head down, did her job, and tried to have fun when she wasn't working. Just like him. He'd never seen another side of her.

That wasn't who she was. Not even half. She didn't argue on the job because there was nothing to argue about. She did what was expected of her, and with an ensemble cast, the responsibilities were divided among a lot of people. He hadn't seen her outside of work because their social circles only crossed on the job.

Now, though, it was just him and her. She had opinions and experience that would make the movie better if she could only get people to listen to her. Mike glanced at her, remembering his attitude at the start of the shoot when she was the one providing all the support. He was glad he'd stepped up, but now he saw what he could have done better. And outside of work? Glinda was a bit of a spitfire with her energy and humor and wit. She spoke up when it was important to her. How had he not noticed until now?

Breakfast was to-go; they passed a diner promising the best cinnamon buns in the state, but Glinda wanted to eat on a beach, so they drove for another half hour until they found a place to pull over. Glinda kept staring at her coffee cup.

"Are you okay?"

"Wishing it wasn't decaf."

"Why did you get it then?"

"Because I'm going to have to sleep today." She stifled a yawn behind her hand. "Sorry. I'm having a good time. Truly."

He understood. At this point he was going more on enthusiasm than energy. "I guess it's time to head back." He wanted to keep going.

"I guess so."

As always, the drive home went faster than the drive out of the city. They were on the freeways just as morning traffic was beginning to ramp up. He passed through the studio gates without incident, and ended up outside Stage Eight before he knew it.

"We're home."

She moved her hand, preparing to pull it away. He grabbed it first. "When can we do this again?" Finding time while they were both filming would be a bitch. He'd sacrifice another night's sleep without hesitation for her, though.

"Are we sure we want to do this?"

"I am. Aren't you?"

"I mean while we're filming. Working together so closely."

They had weeks of primary shooting left. Then they'd get into looping, the audio fixes for the scenes where planes went by overhead, or a car horn beeped in the background. Then pick-ups, where they had to re-shoot segments of scenes. "I am not waiting months before taking you out again."

"Roth may object."

"I don't want to do this to Roth." He leaned in. The first brush of his lips against hers was soft, barely making contact. When Glinda made a little sound in the back of her throat, he kissed her again. Part of his brain noticed the heat of the sunrise on the side of his face, but he was more preoccupied with the warmth of her lips and the lingering taste of cinnamon. Her teeth gently grazed his lower lip, and his blood thrummed to complete attention.

She rocked to her heels, pulling them apart. "Wow."

He'd take that as a compliment. As often as possible. "Well?"

"Well what? I'm a little muddled."

"When can I see you again?"

"As soon as possible."

That he could work with.

Chapter Fifteen

The second unit director claimed to be refreshed after a day off, and ready to start a whole new sequence. Roth aside, Glinda was looking forward to it. Today was the day they were meeting the true stars of *Extinction Level Event*.

They started the day touring Dr. Hanzel's "lab", which was currently under reconstruction. The framework was there, but it had to be converted from a clinic's examination room to a scientist's lab. Carpenters were doing their best to finish the last-minute changes, and painters touched up the raw wooden edges.

Even with daily script changes, learning her lines wasn't the most stressful part of the shoot. Their biggest problem was the crew was still scrambling to catch up. At best, they were a couple days ahead of principal photography. She'd had to change more than once after brushing a wall that still had wet paint on it.

Roth strode to the middle of the set, like a petty dictator surveying his kingdom. "Bring in Amanda!" he ordered.

"Who is Amanda?" she whispered to Mike.

Mike shrugged, his elbow gently brushing her arm.

A four-foot-by-six-foot cage on a low metal cart squeaked as two grips rolled it onto the set. Inside was a full-sized juvenile panda bear with paws the size of dessert plates. She assumed it was going to be a stuffed animal, or fully computer-generated. The black nose stood out on its white face, as did the irregular dark patches around its eyes. It was surprisingly lifelike.

"Mike, Glinda, may I introduce Amanda the Panda. Why don't you say hello?" Roth said.

Glinda moved to get a better look. The black and white fur looked real. "It's not nylon fur, like on a stuffed animal. What is it?"

Mike leaned in too. "I have no idea."

Then Amanda the Panda turned her head and stared at Glinda.

"Holy hell!" she yelled, jumping away from the cage.

Mike laughed the loudest. Glinda didn't care. She kept moving backward until she hit the wall. Amanda's arms went up and she clapped her paws together in lumbering applause.

"Okay, that's pretty good," Glinda admitted.

A high-pitched giggle grew louder as a spiky-haired, geek-t-shirt wearing young woman stepped into view. "Hi. I'm Teresa Gomez. This is Amanda. I can't believe you fell for that." She fiddled with the remote control in her hands, and the animatronic panda waved.

"I'm Glinda Crawford. This is cool. Did you make it?"

"Nah, but I found her. We generally prefer CGI over robotics, but we had this bad girl in storage. A little dusting, a little battery recharge and, despite the ancient technology, we were good to go. I've been playing with her for a couple days to get the hang of the controls. I think we'll be fine. I'll be working her off-camera, but it would be best if we could keep her actions to a minimum," she said.

She and Mike took a moment to examine their co-star more closely. Teresa pointed out the articulating digits in the paws, and the independent eye movements. Glinda was amazed at the detail, down to the lashes. "It's really perfect."

"There may be one big problem. Literally. I'm supposed to lift Amanda out of the cage and sit her on the examination table. How much does she weigh?" Mike asked.

"About a hundred pounds. It's the motors and the skeleton. The padding itself is lightweight."

"As a deadlift? That'll be fun."

"Amanda can help with that." Teresa opened the cage door. "I should be able to have her put her paws on your shoulders and lean forward until she tilts. She'll fall forward into you. Then you're lifting with your legs. Will that help?"

"Immensely. Let's give it a practice run." He raised his arms and bounced up and down in a couple squats, reached for the ceiling. The hem of his T-shirt slipped out of his waistband, revealing his lower abs and a thick line of black hair heading south.

The crew cleared the set to give him the room he'd need for the maneuver. Glinda stepped to the end of the examination table, and handed him the white lab coat he'd be wearing. "If you're going to do it, you should see how restricted you are." She crossed to the door to the lab, where she'd be entering for the shot.

Mike flicked the simple catch on the door. "We're going to have to change that. A real bear would be able to swipe that mechanism with its claws."

"Noted," Roth said. "Whenever you're ready, Mike."

"Okay, here we go," Mike said to the bear.

Both furry front legs went up and rested atop Mike's biceps. "Nice. Good bear." Amanda tilted forward, and the bear's head hit his chest. It took him two tries to get a grip on the bear that still allowed him to find some stability. His boots had soft rubber soles, meaning he couldn't simply slide them across the tile floor to find better balance. Instead, he dragged them. Glinda winced at the wicked squeaks they gave every time he shifted his feet. "You're a heavy one, aren't you?" He dropped fractionally before he hefted the bear and set it on his hip, then transferred it to the examination table.

Glinda crossed the room. "Are we certain she's not symptomatic, Doctor?"

"This girl is perfectly healthy, and our best hope for finding a cure. She must be carrying antibodies in her bloodstream. Grab me a needle from that tray over there, Captain."

They went through the motions of drawing blood from the bear while Roth watched them through a monitor. "Okay, that'll work well. Can we have some powder on the floor behind the table for Mike's shoes?" he asked a production assistant.

The kid rushed to find powder, and three others put Amanda back in her cage and added a second lock.

"Let's do it again for real."

Glinda waited for them to reset the entire set. She overheard Mike talking to Teresa.

"Can you get her paws any higher? Move them to my shoulders?" he asked. "The weight is okay, but if she can prevent herself from tipping back, it would be easier."

"No problem," the tech assured him.

"Action!"

Mike unclipped Amanda's cage. "Hello, beautiful girl." The legs began to slide up and in. Its head slowly dropped at the same time Mike grabbed under the hind legs, and waited for the bear to shift. Glinda could see when it happened; the bear tipped forward the slightest bit, and it shifted its center of balance. Mike bent his knees. "Here we go," he announced.

"That's enough, girl. You don't have to give me a throat hug."

That's when Glinda realized the panda's grip had moved past his shoulders, and its paws were on his collarbones. And they were still inching up. "You can stop any time now, panda," he repeated louder.

The articulating fingers the technician had been so proud of curled into claws biting into the base of Mike's neck. Glinda had done her research when she accepted the role; she knew pandas had thumbs. She hadn't expected one press into Mike's carotid artery and cut off blood flow to his brain. Because of the angle, the bear's other paw pressed into his windpipe, choking off his oxygen supply.

"Kill the bear! Kill the bear!" she yelled. To Teresa Gomez, to Roth, to anyone who could help.

"I'm sorry, I can't. The remote control isn't working."

Mike gasped, then dropped to his knees. The bear hit the ground with a thump, but it didn't let go. It fell to its side, Mike still locked in its grip.

Once he started to fall, Glinda didn't waste a moment. She raced across the laboratory set and dropped to her knees beside him. Mike wasn't fooling around; after their adventures together, she recognized his mortal danger face.

First, she tried to pull the bear's front leg away by yanking at the joint. "Let go of him, you bitch!" Her hands slipped off the immovable limb and she ended up throwing herself backward. She scrambled closer again and managed to wrap her fingers around Amanda's thumb. It didn't budge; in fact, she could feel the grip around Mike's neck getting tighter. "What the hell are you doing?"

A frustrated cry came from off camera. "Nothing. It won't respond." Glinda could see technician pressing buttons and flipping switches, but nothing stopped Amanda the Panda. Teresa whacked the remote-control unit against a pole, then tried again. "Still nothing," the tech reported.

"How do we stop her?" Glinda asked. Mike was gasping now. Tears leaked from his eyes. His cheeks puffed out as he tried to draw a breath, but Amanda the Panda's assault was relentless.

"I can't. Access is through the chest," Teresa shouted.

Which meant they couldn't reach the battery to pull it and kill the power while it was bear-hugging Mike to death.

"Then think of something!" she grunted. Glinda wasn't going to stand idly by and watch her leading man be strangled to death.

Mike was struggling less now. His hands kept slipping on the fur.

Glinda braced her feet on the panda's shoulders. They were wide enough to stand on, so she had no fear of her boots slipping off. She weaved her fingers together, cupped her hands under the bear's muzzle and jaw. And pulled.

The muscles in her shoulders burned. She felt the bear's metal endoskeleton bruising her hands but she didn't stop. She stiffened her thighs and began a slow, steady ascent against the mechanical resistance.

A hydraulic whine seemed to come out of the bear's mouth. The head came up fractionally, and Glinda could see the front legs retracting the same amount. She pulled harder. She heard Mike suck in a breath of air, wheeze an exhale, then take a stronger breath.

"Glinda, stop. You're breaking the bear," Roth ordered from the sidelines, where he hadn't moved a muscle to help.

"The bear is breaking Mike," she ground out through gritted teeth. She tried to adjust her grip, but the second she stopped pulling, the hydraulics kicked back in and she lost the breathing room she'd gained. She'd have to keep the pressure on until Mike was free or...

The head came up another inch. Mike managed to wedge his hand under the panda's left thumb, and was pushing it away with both hands. Glinda heard him suck in more air. "Don't let go, Mike" she said in warning.

"Can't get it off," Mike gasped.

"Don't damage it. We can't replace that bear," Roth warned.

Well, she couldn't replace Mike, either. And she liked him better. Glinda shifted her foot slightly, took a deep breath, and pulled for all she was worth. The mechanical whine increased as the machine fought against her interference. "Die, Fuzzy, die!" she yelled, digging deep for one last spurt of energy. Then she heard the sound of ripping fabric. The whine stopped.

The next thing she knew, Glinda was flying. She hit the floor, executed a backward shoulder roll Matti West would have been proud of, and ended up on her ass with a panda head in her lap. She tossed it aside and crawled back to Mike.

He'd managed to pry the bear paws far enough apart to escape the mechanized grip. He propped himself against the lab cupboards opposite the examination table. He gave the beheaded panda torso a vicious kick.

She collapsed beside him. "You okay?" Obviously, he wasn't. Self-inflicted scratches marred his throat. She could see bruises forming, and he was still coughing. But he was breathing, so that was an improvement from a minute ago.

"Yep."

Glinda gave the decapitated panda a kick as well. She wrapped her arm around Mike's shoulders while he caught his breath. "Four days without a workplace incident, Mosley. This one's on you. Again," she whispered in his ear.

"I love you so much right now," he said with a laugh.

"I know," she replied.

A tremor ran through him as she held him, so she hugged him a little tighter. Glinda thought the flash flood had been bad; this had come so much closer. The crew cracked jokes while the medic checked Mike out. He shot the crew a thumbs-up, but she knew he was shakier than he looked. What happened may have looked funny but it was no joke. Mike had come close to dying.

Throughout it all, she watched Roth throw a tantrum behind the windrow of cables and wires. They had a few seconds of blessed silence before he started up again. "Do you have any idea what you've done, Glinda? How much you've cost this production? That bear was one of a kind, and it cost more than your contract! Now we're delayed until it can be fixed," he ranted.

"If it can be fixed," Teresa added morosely. The technician cradled Amanda's head. Wires poked out of the neck, and thin, silver oil leaked out of torn tubes on either side of the bear's neck. "I can't believe you decapitated Amanda!"

"The cost overrun on this is going to destroy the budget. I guarantee you it'll be taken out of your pay," Roth continued.

Mike stirred, mumbling something about taking care of Roth. Glinda patted his muscular thigh. "I've got this one." She climbed to her feet, wincing at the pinch in her back. She took two steps to get right in Roth's face. Since they were the same height, she didn't have to look up to go eye to eye with him. "Left or right?" she asked.

"What?"

"Which testicle do you want me to leave intact? The last director that tried to kill us lost his right one, but I didn't ask first. This time I'll take your preference into consideration, therefore I need to know—left or right?" Glinda was past caring. There were business priorities and there were basic human priorities. If Robert Roth couldn't get them straight, she'd teach him. Painfully, if necessary. "And where the hell is the ambulance for Mike?" She pointed at a male P.A. holding a tablet standing beside the director. "You. Personally. Go outside and wait for it. Bring them back here as soon as they arrive. Now!"

The director opened his mouth, which was his last mistake. "This was an accident!"

That was enough to set her off again. "The panda, yes. But if you try to stop him for going for help, Robert, I'll make the choice for you." She turned to her next target. "Teresa, get some of the P.A.s to take Amanda's body to wherever you work and see if you can reattach her head." She sensed Mike move behind her, so she whirled and crouched beside him. "You don't move unless they are loading you into the ambulance. Clear?"

"You're gorgeous when you're angry." Mike's voice was quiet. She barely heard it over the rest of the bustle on the set, but she did hear it. And she saw the way he smiled at her. He meant it.

Glinda caught a glimpse of herself in one of the stainless-steel cabinet doors Mike was resting against. Her hair, which was supposed to be pulled into a military-approved bun, had escaped its pins, and her curls stuck out in all directions, giving her the effect of being a blonde Medusa. Her cheeks were bright red, like somebody had dotted them with a rouge stick without bothering to blend the color. And she had a spatter of panda grease across her chin.

"Great, you've got brain damage from oxygen deprivation," she muttered.

He said something. It was too quiet to hear, but the look he wore said it was important. She leaned in. "What was that?"

"No chance," he said. Then he lifted his hand, threaded it into her hair, and pulled her in for a kiss.

She should stop him. Roth was looking for an excuse to get rid of her, and this was as unprofessional as—wow, that was good. It didn't have the same determination as the kiss they'd shared the morning before, but it was just as sweet. Just as deep.

And like last time, she had to end it no matter how much she wanted it to go on.

Glinda pulled away the slightest bit. Mike let her go. His dark brown eyes sparked with emotion, but they were firmly fixed on her, and she was so close nobody else could see the urgency on his face. "We don't have time for games," he whispered.

"EMTs are coming!" somebody behind them yelled.

She stood slowly and made room for the medics with their first aid kits. Roth was on his phone, shouting, and waving his arms even though the person on the other end of the line couldn't see him. Yeah, she was going to pay for threatening to castrate him. She fished her own phone out of her pocket and hit speed-dial. "Hi, it's Glinda Crawford. Is Fiona free? There's been another accident."

Chapter Sixteen

Glinda was hiding from him. She hadn't come to the hospital with him. She'd stayed behind to deal with Robert Roth and the rest of the studio and union people. He tracked down Erin Thorne and got a full recap of events after he left. Apparently, she'd taken the attack on him as a personal insult and had gone on an offensive that left Roth shaking in his boots. His throat hurt from laughing when Erin relayed Glinda's threat of "I just ripped the head off a terminator bear, do you really think you can take me?"

He swung by her trailer after he'd been released from the hospital, but he'd missed her and he was too sore to track her down that day. Now he was parked outside her house with coffee, but she wasn't there either. They needed to talk, and not just about what to do regarding Robert Roth and the fate of *Extinction Level Event*. She had been home earlier; the flowerpots on either side of her front door were freshly watered. But her car was gone and she wasn't answering her phone.

"Hi, Fiona. Thanks for calling back so quickly. I'm trying to get a hold of Glinda before our meeting this morning. Do you know where she is?" Roth wanted Glinda gone. Completely replaced. They needed to discuss strategy.

"Maybe she's wandering around in a daze after the lip lock you put on her yesterday."

"You heard about that, huh?" He was surprised there hadn't been a photo making the rounds. He'd heard eye-witness interviews on several news shows and radio stations, but apparently, the panda attack and subsequent kiss had happened so quickly nobody had a chance to film anything.

"Yes. What were you thinking?"

"That I almost died and before I went, I really, really needed to kiss Glinda. Did she say anything to you?"

"She said lots. Most of it at a thousand words a minute so I didn't understand any of it. Is this going to mess you two up on screen? Your production already has enough problems."

"You're not kidding. No, it's not going to be a problem." He'd make sure of that.

"I told her come to my office first and we'd drive to the apocalypse together. I want her to meet a couple of our lawyers first. Everybody's coming to today's meeting, including Lucie Caruso herself and two executive producers. We're going discuss the safety issues on this disaster of a project, and square everything else away once and for all. Wait for us in the lobby. I need you two to be on the same page. Especially since Roth is claiming Glinda maliciously and deliberately destroyed a half-million-dollar model."

"It was deliberate, and I'm glad it was, but malicious? Amanda the Panda was trying to kill me. And not movie kill me. Actually kill me."

"Is there any chance Glinda could have taken any other action?"

"No. I literally couldn't breathe. She saved me, Fiona. My medical records will attest to that. I'd hope a bear would come second to my life. You may also want to note Roth took no action at all."

"I already have the email you sent. We'll discuss it before we go up. Don't be late. We don't need to give them any more ammunition."

The Grover Building was an anomaly; a low, three-story wood and windows structure rather than a steel and glass high-rise. Mike figured the natural materials made the legal predators inside feel more at home. Fiona's six-figure ride cruised to the curb, and Glinda hopped out dressed in a stark, red business suit that was severe enough to make him look twice. Gone was the easy-going actress. This woman was out for blood and wasn't afraid to show it.

It was sexy as hell.

Fiona looked equally impressive. He felt underdressed in his slacks, shirt and sports jacket. "We have some time," Fiona said. "What do you want out of this meeting?"

"Not to get fired. To get some kind of safety protocols in action, not just on paper. And for the director to show up," Glinda said.

"I'm not worried about the first one, but I'd like for Glinda not to be fired. The same on the other two things she mentioned," he added.

Fiona nodded. "Glinda's in the shit because of the bear. Threatening Roth didn't help matters, but I think we can chalk that up to extreme emotional distress. I have to warn you two, this is not good. Most of it isn't your fault, but I'm hearing rumors of putting the entire production into turnaround. You've developed a cursed reputation. They're afraid to put in any more money."

"Decapitating the bear was an accident," Glinda protested. "Accident-ish. I wouldn't have done it if Mike's life hadn't been on the line. It's not like I threw a temper-tantrum and took it out on a multi-million-dollar camera."

No, that was Roth, Mike had heard. If the powers-that-be were serious about cost overruns, Roth had bumped Glinda out of the hot seat.

Glasses sat at each spot around the table with pitchers of water in the middle. The production team had arrived first and chosen the chairs that backed against the wall, leaving them squinting into the sunlight coming through the windows. Fiona walked past the empty seats and pulled the blinds closed, cutting off their psychological intimidation ploy before the meeting had even begun.

Two chairs were empty when they arrived. As he looked around the table, Mike realized they were for Lucie Caruso and her representative. He was as shocked as Glinda when Antonia Caruso came through the door.

"I apologize for being late. I trust my explanation will explain my tardiness, as well as several other recent events," the Italian woman in her late fifties said.

She looked like a director, Mike thought. She had a commanding air, confidence bordering on arrogance, and a voice that brooked no argument. Her gray hair was streaked with black, and her jacket—no cape, he corrected himself—looked like a painter's palette. He'd been in the same room as her for five seconds and he already knew he'd never want to cross her.

"My daughter, Lucie, is very ill. She has been admitted to hospital in Rome. We had hoped she would be well enough to work, but she is not."

That put the question of continuing work on the picture to bed. It was the final nail in the coffin. He shared a look with Fiona, but didn't show any other reaction. He wouldn't be the first actor to have a project fall apart, and he wouldn't be the last. It didn't change the fact that it sucked.

"However," Antonia continued, "with such a big investment already having been made, we have been looking at options. Lucie and I have been watching the dailies as they've come in. We have a lot of footage to work with."

They should. Mike hadn't discovered any rhyme or reason to the order of the scenes they'd shot, aside from the fact they were – with one noticeable exception – panda-free. The second-unit directors had pushed hard to complete the action sequences first, but they didn't have any plot-heavy sequences filmed to tie them together.

"Therefore, I will be stepping in to finish principal photography."

Glinda stiffened beside him. He heard the intake of breath through her nose but the general din which erupted covered the sound for anyone not sitting next to her. He flashed back to their meal at Limelight, where she'd gone into raptures at the idea of working with Antonia Caruso; now it was happening.

"We will be taking another pass at the script to reflect these changes, and to salvage what we can from both previous drafts. We intend to resume production in a week."

"What about Roth's accusations about Glinda?" he asked.

"Mr. Roth will no longer be working on the production."

Even better. He tuned out the rest of the meeting, trusting Fiona to fill him in on any of the details he missed. The important part of Antonia's announcement meant that he wasn't working for a week. Neither was Glinda. Which meant he had time to take her on a proper date. Preferably more than one.

Amanda the Panda had died a noble death.

Chapter Seventeen

Her head was spinning. She wasn't fired. She wasn't even in trouble. Of course, the accountants disapproved of Amanda's decapitation, but since it was cheaper than the life insurance policy they had on Mike, they didn't complain too hard.

Even bigger news was Antonia Caruso. Antonia Caruso, the every-award-winning director was going to be directing her. Her. In a movie. Which she was starring in. It was every professional dream she'd ever had. The thought took Glinda's breath away.

She barely had the mental bandwidth to think of what was going on with Mike.

He didn't kiss her on the front steps of the Grover Building, but the look in his eyes said he wanted to do. "This is good news. My calendar is clear for the next week while they tweak the script. So is yours. Where would you like to go for dinner, or shall I pick a place? You know what? Never mind. I'll pick a place. Wear something nice."

He said goodbye, telling her he had plans to make, and Fiona came around with her car. Her agent yammered for first few minutes of their drive, but Glinda didn't realize she'd stopped until she noticed the car had stopped moving. The shade of the palm tree sheltered her from the midday heat, helping her bring her mind into focus.

"Are you seeing Mike Mosley?" Fiona asked without preamble.

"Yes."

"Do you think that is wise?"

"Not unless you know something about him I don't know."

"I don't want you to get hurt. Especially while you're filming with him," Fiona said. "I stay out of my clients' private lives until it interferes with our business. You two are having enough problems professionally without adding romantic entanglements into the mix."

"I appreciate your concern, Fiona, but we're adults. We can handle it, and unless it does impact our jobs, I'd prefer to keep anything between me and Mike private."

Her words earned her a second glance. "When you first started with me, you would have asked if you should break up with him."

It was true. She would have asked. But not only did she not want to ask for permission, she didn't want to imagine him not being around.

"That was a long time ago, Fiona. I'm not that kid anymore. Besides, I'm not making this decision based on how it might impact my career. It's too important to me. I want to see Mike again, and I'm going to."

"I'm not saying you can't. But I'm glad to hear you're serious about him. You deserve it."

Glinda didn't think she was ready to talk about how serious she was. It was too soon. Instead, she changed the conversation. "Speaking of seeing, what did you do to make Roth's nude scene go away?"

Her agent laughed and put the car back in gear. "Not much. Your immovable 'no' shut him down hard. He had one of the lawyers attached to the project call me, but your contract was crystal clear. He's done it before. This time he got his hand slapped. I'm sure he would have tried something else with you except—"

"The entire crew witnessed me rip the head off a rogue cyborg panda."

"Yes. I doubt you'll be having trouble with anybody for a while. So, about Mike?"

"I'll handle it."

Glinda's version of handling it consisted of cycling through her walk-in closet three times to find the perfect outfit for a night of unknown possibilities. She settled on a baby blue dress with long sleeves and no back, silver shoes, and a matching clutch. It took an hour and half a can of hair product to ensure her blonde curls fell in natural, perfect waves. She could be drastically overdressed, but she wouldn't know it until Mike showed up on her doorstep.

When he did, she breathed a sigh of relief. He was decked out in a slim fit, black suit, black belt, white shirt, and a copper tie that did amazing things to his deep, brown eyes. Wherever they were headed, they were going to be the best-looking couple there.

Cosmo's was a rising star in the Los Angeles dining scene. The established Greek restaurant had recently changed hands and reopened with a new chef and a new menu. The maître d' showed them to a secluded table with a view of the city skyline. Mike had chosen well; they offered several non-meat options in case she was in a vegetarian mood. And everything else if she wasn't.

"Did your cousin's daughter like her present?" Mike asked.

"It was a pink unicorn. I'm the best second-aunt ever." She hadn't defaulted to what a generic four-year old would think was cool. Laurie had specifically asked for a herd of stuffed unicorns in different colors. Glinda had drawn pink; Dory had drawn black.

"Have you thought about your own? Kids?"

Glinda did not choke on her wine, but it was close. It wasn't a typical second date question, but it made sense. They'd known each other for a while; that skipped a lot of steps. "Yes, and yes. Sooner rather than later. The clock is ticking. How about you?"

"Yes. It's time I settled."

"Settled?" Glinda concentrated on resetting her brain. He couldn't know that having people "settle" for her was a hot button. She'd had three long-term acting roles and, in each one, the production team's original choice had been unavailable. She'd been everyone's second pick, and some of them hadn't been shy about letting her know it. *The Bamboo Mountain*, or *Extinction Level Event* or whatever title it ended up with, was the first time she'd been directly approached for a role. Roth's barb about not being able to choose his own actress had struck deeper than she let show.

"Ten years ago would have been better, but I still want kids."

"Oh, like settle down," she said.

"Exactly. I think you lower your expectations as you get older. The One when you're twenty isn't necessarily going to be The One when you're thirty. Or forty."

"Do you really think that's settling? I don't think my expectations have dropped. I think they've become more realistic. Not to mention, my priorities have changed. That changes what I want out of a partner."

"That's true too. You start looking under the skin at other things." Mike must have sensed his comment was not well received because he quickly added. "Not that I'm saying you don't have great skin."

"Thank you. I moisturize," she joked.

"Seriously, Glinda, did I say something?"

"No, I misunderstood when you said settle down. I heard something else." She scooted closer to him in the semi-circular booth. "Not that we're there yet, but it's good to know we're on the same page."

She raised her eyes, her hint for him to bend closer so she could kiss him. He caught it, and seconds later she couldn't remember what they'd been talking about. If it weren't for the server interrupting them, it would have gone on longer.

"I've always wanted to try stuffed grape leaves. Have you had them?" Mike asked after the waiter recommended them.

"Me, too, and no, I haven't. Do you want to split an order?"

They shared their desserts too, ordering two because the decision was too hard.

"What's next? Another drive up the coast?" She liked the way the last one ended. Even better, this time they didn't have to go to work in the morning.

"No. At least, not yet. Do you like jazz?"

"I don't have a lot of experience with it, but I like what I've heard."

"Excellent."

The club he took her to sounded vaguely familiar, but it wasn't on her radar. It was old Los Angeles, with a fully restored Art Deco vibe, from the rounded windows and front entrance, to the font on the drink menu. Again, he arranged a private table. She knew it wasn't embarrassment to be seen with her; he was trying to ensure they had the privacy they wanted. It was a fine line to walk, and he was doing an admirable job.

"Do you come here often?"

"Often enough if they have somebody I want to hear. My music collection is eclectic but I have a few favorites. Eloise Bright is one of them. Wait until you hear her voice."

The house lights went down and the stage lights went up. A stunning black woman took the stage in a floor-length evening dress. Then she began to sing, and Glinda completely forgot about how she looked.

"Holy...wow!" she exclaimed when the first set ended. She'd been utterly transported. Her back ached from leaning forward and holding herself perfectly still in an effort not to miss a single note.

Mike had slipped her hand into his, and had yet to let go. While the band took their break, he tugged her closer. "I take it you liked her."

"Very much."

"Want to meet her?"

Glinda hesitated. "Yes, but I'd rather sit here with you," she answered honestly. She got as big a thrill out of meeting artists she admired as the next person, but tonight she was loath to let anyone intrude. Mike didn't seem to mind her refusal. He draped his arm over the back of her chair, and they snuggled—as much as two people in separate seats could—through Eloise Bright's second set and her encore. He was constantly touching her shoulder, running a lock of hair through his fingers, rubbing her back. Every touch built on the last until she could barely concentrate on the music.

The cut on Glinda's foot was healed, but the ache from wrenching her ankle remained. Wedging it into a pair of sexy heels had done wonders for her fashion sense, but her foot was killing her. She walked a little slower as they returned to his car, and Mike noticed her limp.

"Is your foot hurting you?" he asked.

"I made a poor footwear selection."

"Why didn't you say anything?"

"I was having a good time." Before she could speak, he scooped her up into his arms and strode across the parking lot. "Mike!" it came out as a squeal. "What do you think you're doing?"

"Keeping you from re-injuring your foot. And pressing you against my manly chest in an attempt to seduce you. How's it working?"

She patted the firm pec under her hand. "Pretty well. But I look like an idiot."

"I'd like to hear anyone tell you that." But he set her down. They were at his car already.

She could get used to driving through Los Angeles at night with the roof down. There was something illicit in being out in the dark with a handsome man when she should be at home, asleep in her bed.

The ride to her place was much too short. Unlike their last drive, Mike didn't take the scenic route. He pulled into her driveway and parked. Then he stared at her. "You look beautiful in the moonlight."

"Would you like to come in for a drink?"

Chapter Eighteen

It was a wonderful kind of torture, being next to Glinda all night but only being able to give her the most casual caresses in public. He'd seen her in varying stages of undress, but having thirty or forty crewmembers around took all the fun out of it. He wanted to strip her out of her heart-stopping dress and have the whole sight to himself.

"Mike?"

Shit, he'd been so busy staring at her that he'd missed what she said. "What was that?"

"Do you want to come in for a drink?"

"Yes."

The flowers in the pots he'd noticed earlier were as perky as ever, but the white blooms had closed for the night. Her front door was a dark green that was almost black in the shadows.

He entered a massive foyer, full of light wood flooring, cream walls and flowers on every available surface. Glinda dumped her purse on a table and pointed through an archway. "Bar's that way. I'll be right there."

Her living room looked fresh out of a decorating magazine, only lived in. A cashmere blanket was pooled in the corner of the leather couch, and a novel was open and face-down on the polished coffee table beside a mug, centered on a coaster. The vivid paintings displayed on the wall were good, but seemed amateur and out of place. The living room flowed into the dining room, which ended with French doors leading to a deck and pool lit with a soft, emerald glow.

Glinda floated out of the kitchen in bare feet, her heels abandoned, painted toes sparkling against the white tile. She held two wine glasses in one hand, and a bottle in the other. "If you haven't chosen something from the cabinet, I have wine."

"I don't want wine." Or scotch, or water.

"Thank God. The bottle's empty." She set them on the island as she passed by, and flew into his arms.

His hands slid up the barely-there material covering her arms, then down her back, everywhere he could touch that would draw her closer to him. Her lips touched the point of his chin, then the corner of his mouth.

He couldn't handle the teasing. He lifted her to her toes and then aimed his mouth straight at hers. Her fresh taste burst through him, driving away his need to come up for air until his lungs burned. "I can't get enough of you."

"I know the feeling."

With a few little nudges, he could slide her dress straps off her shoulders. If he added a couple gentle tugs, it would be pooling at her feet. He wanted that. Desperately. She'd crawled inside his head faster than anyone he'd ever met. He needed to be close to her.

"This is happening very fast."

She pulled away from him, just a little, and it hurt. "It is."

"Are we sure we want to do this?"

"I am. Are you?"

"I definitely want to do this. Are we rushing? With all we've been through, are we sure we're starting out the right way? Should we give ourselves time to decide if we really want to take this step while we're working together?" It would complicate things even if everything went perfectly.

"Are you trying to talk me out of this?" Glinda asked.

"No." If anything, he wanted to talk her into it. He just didn't want her to have any regrets. He needed her to be as certain as he was.

She took another step back. "But it's something you are concerned about it." When he didn't deny it, she continued. "So let's hold off and not rush things."

"I'm not turning you down."

"Of course not. I'm incredible. But easing back would give us both time to think."

"Okay." It was what he wanted. Kind of. The rest of him wanted to find out what the inside of her bedroom looked like.

"I'm still going to make you kiss me good night," she added.

If that was all he was getting, he was going to make it count.

Chapter Nineteen

Thank God for BOB. Mike may have left her hanging on the verge of orgasm after two kisses that made her panties spontaneously combust, but her friendly, neighborhood vibrator had come through. Three times, because that is how long it took her to come down after Mike got her revved up.

He had looked amazing in his suit. There was nothing like a well-dressed man, unless he was totally undressed. By the sounds of things, he was going to make her wait for that.

After a few hours of sleep, part of her was secretly glad. She didn't regret being with Mike, but she was having second thoughts about doing it while they were still working together. She was certain what she felt for him wouldn't fade in a month. But that didn't mean they had to stay away from each other.

Glinda puttered into her kitchen, wrapped nape to ankle in an Egyptian cotton robe, snagged a cup of coffee from the waiting pod machine, and continued out to her pool deck. She stared at the cell phone she'd brought along, but she wasn't up to that yet. She needed a plan of action, but first she needed caffeine.

She sighed. She was being irrational, and she knew it. The fact she knew she knew didn't stop the circular argument from playing on a continuous loop in her head. She needed to break it, and the best person to do it was several states away.

"You can do this, Glinda. Work the problem," she said to herself. She plucked a sprig of rosemary and began doing a twisted version of "he loves me, he loves me not" on it.

One needle-like leaf went to the side of her coffee cup. "Pro, he respects me. On and off set."

One went to the right. "He won't be the one being called a slut when this comes out."

That was as far as she got. Did she really want to be one more actress known for hooking up with her co-star? That never ended well. The massive racks of tabloids at the grocery store proved it every week. Then again, she had never lived her social life in the headlines; there was no reason she had to start doing so now. Glinda frowned. "I shouldn't have to worry about what other people may say about who I date," she said to herself, her voice full of bravado.

She almost believed it.

She stood up and looked at her reflection in the patio door. "One more time for those in the back, Crawford." She pointed at her own face. "You don't owe anyone an explanation about who you date. Now go get that Greek god of sex, drugs, and rock and roll, girl!"

Glinda held up her right hand, and slapped it with her left. "Self high-five!"

She drained her coffee and stormed into her bedroom, looking for the casual outfit to end all outfits. Then she paused. She needed to do two things first.

The first was easily solved with a quick call to Fiona. The woman had contacts everywhere; tracking down a special request item and arranging delivery was a snap. The second required pleading, threats, and a bribe that was going to cost her big time, but she got what she needed.

Her white baseball jersey was new, but not unworn. She'd been to four Dodgers games in the last few years, mostly with visiting family members. She'd never been in the good seats where she wouldn't have to endure beer spilled down her back and popcorn showers when the home team made a great play. She'd worn the cap often enough that the brim was broken in. That hat and a pair of sunglasses made up her favourite disguise when she didn't want to be recognized. It didn't always work, but really, how closely did people look at the person next to them pumping gas?

She ensured the envelope Fiona sent over was tucked safely into the glove box, pulled the cap a little tighter onto her head, and strode up the sidewalk to Mike's house.

His doorbell was a buzzer to his unit. She leaned on the button a second time. Apparently, he wasn't home.

Which messed with all her plans. How could she take him out if he were already out? Glinda knew she'd been unreasonably lucky to find an afternoon home game on a weekday. There wouldn't be another that season. She should have planned better. Now her options were to hand out even more markers in an attempt to track Mike down before the opening pitch or to—

"Glinda?" Mike stood in the entrance, shirtless, with a pair of fleece shorts slung low on his hips. He was covered in sweat and a water bottle dangled from one hand.

"Um. Ah…" Her entire vocabulary had fled.

"Why are you here? Are you okay? Why didn't you call?"

She didn't call because she didn't want to lose her nerve. His questions weren't helping her self-confidence either. "Mike Mosley, would you like to go out on a date with me? I'd like to take you to a baseball game today, if you don't have other plans." This was a lot tougher than she expected. Being the guy wasn't for sissies.

"Didn't we discuss that I expected to pay on our dates?"

"Yeah, well, you didn't ask me out on a second date, so I had to take matters into my own hands. Are you in, or are you out?"

He didn't say a word.

Perhaps she'd misread things. Yes, he'd taken her out, but it had been very low profile. Just the two of them, with nobody else to see. Maybe she wasn't the only one worried about going public.

Glinda blew her bangs off her forehead. "If you've changed your mind about wanting to see me again, you're allowed to do that. But don't be a dick about it. Would you like to go to a ball game this afternoon or not?" She had to remember that embarrassment wasn't fatal. Only the two of them would know if he turned her down flat. She didn't think he'd tell anyone else; she'd never seen him do anything that petty.

But she would have to face him every day on the set knowing he thought she wasn't worth another date. Which, while embarrassing to the point of absolute humiliation, would not kill her. Maybe just a piece of her soul.

Now she was being dramatic.

Mike continued to stare.

"I'd very much like to go out with you this afternoon. I need to take a shower first. I was in the gym and saw you through the window as I was headed upstairs. Come in."

At least he *sounded* interested.

His place was about the same age as hers, but while she had gone for light, bright rooms, Mike had decorated in dark wood and warm colors. A navy accent wall in a gray living room, a burgundy one in his beige dining room that flowed into his kitchen with its espresso cabinets and dark stone counter. "Can I get you a drink while you wait?"

"Water, please."

He handed her a bottle and disappeared. Glinda heard water running and decided to level the playing field a little. Mike knew much more about her than she knew about him, and he'd been in her house.

There was a recent picture of him and an older man hanging on a dining room wall. Another of him and the same man and a woman when Mike was a kid. He and the woman had the same eyes, so Glinda assumed she was his mother, but she didn't see any other pictures of her.

The glass frames in the kitchen cupboard doors revealed thick plates, heavy mugs, and sturdy glasses. Mike had a half-empty fruit bowl on the counter with three oranges and a green apple, a crock with utensils, and a toaster. Aside from some crumbs near the toaster, everything was clean and put away.

Glinda flashed to her dish pantry, which had four different china patterns, one for each season, in addition to her every day dishes. Plus, her two afternoon tea sets. Mike was a man's man, and her home screamed girly girl. They didn't share a lot of middle ground.

She shook off the negative thought. They had baseball in common. Acting. They both liked his convertible. She really liked his convertible; he'd barely fit in her crossover.

"I'm ready."

She yelped. She hadn't heard him return; the thick carpet in the hall had muffled his footsteps. He was in jeans and a t-shirt, and had a blue Dodgers cap on. That was all she had time to notice before he stepped closer and placed his hand on the side of his face. She froze as he leaned in for a kiss. A very deep, hot kiss that had her holding on for dear life.

"Hello," Mike said. "That was the greeting I wanted to give you, but I was all sweaty."

Now she felt better. "I don't mind sweaty kisses. Although, your fresh from the shower kiss was pretty good too." To date, all her kisses with Mike were impressive, but to judge fairly, she needed a bigger sample. A much bigger sample.

"How did you know I liked baseball?"

"Everybody likes baseball." She'd guessed. He didn't talk sports on set, but she'd seen him in at least two different caps, including the one he was currently wearing.

"How did you get tickets to today's game?"

"I'm just that good, Mike. Are you doubting me?"

He kissed her again. Just a quick peck. "Never. Do we have to leave now?"

She tried insisting she should drive because it was her date, but that argument only got her a pat on the bum before Mike steered her to his car. Parking was its usual zoo, but they managed to get to their seats before the national anthem. Glinda ensured they had everything they needed—programs, popcorn, drinks— and she settled in for an afternoon of watching hot men in tight pants run the bases.

Glinda followed the plays, but she spent as much time people-watching as she did player-watching. When she noticed Mike had also seen the family of five, all with Dodger blue hair, she nudged his arm. "For the record, I don't like baseball that much," she told him.

"I do."

"You've dyed your hair blue?"

"Don't be ridiculous. It was purple. And a wig." He laughed. "I'm serious."

She liked the way he made her laugh. He did it all the time; she felt better just being around him.

"I like that you make me laugh," he continued, like he had heard her thoughts. His voice dropped low, though there was nobody nearby to overhear. "I like that you surprised me with a date, even though you didn't let me pay for it. I really like how adorable you look in your fan gear." His thumb stroked the back of her hand, sending tingles up her spine. He tugged gently on her hand, pulling her in.

Every time he kissed her, it was different. The *don't kill the director*, the *hot, sweet good night*, the *glad to see you at my door*. The *I'm glad your mine*, though, blew the others right out the water. It started with a teasing nibble on her lower lip, moved into a full lip press, and then it got really good. The soft pressure stole her breath as Mike filled her senses. The gentle touch of his tongue made her moan. It was a damned shame they were in the middle of a stadium.

A roar went up from the crowd. "I think we missed a play," she said

Mike turned his head and nodded, indicating she should look in that direction. "We were the play."

The big screen above the digital scoreboard wasn't showing the game. They had the "kiss cam" logo in the corner, and her and Mike in the middle of the heart frame. Her smile, left over from the kiss, didn't falter. Mike slipped his arm behind her shoulders, and she waved in the direction of where the camera should be.

The crowd roared again before the kiss cam found its next victims.

"The news is out now," Mike said.

"Are you worried about that?"

"No. You?"

"Not so much." It was only a little lie. A little razzing would be worth what was developing. The kiss cam returned, hoping to catch them unaware in another smooch. This time they both waved at the camera. A thought popped into her head. "Are you worried? Are we moving too fast here?"

"I hope not. I don't think we've gotten started."

When play resumed, all attention returned to the battle on the diamond, even Mike's. She tried, but she was too busy making plans for a hell of a post-game show. "What inning are we in again? Can we wait for three more innings?"

Chapter Twenty

Four extra innings made the game run into full rush hour traffic, which added hours to their date. The longer timeframe wasn't a problem in and of itself—Mike liked every minute he spent with Glinda—but he would have preferred to spend them at his place, or her place. Anywhere but in a crowd of forty-eight thousand people with a cameraman who thought they provided an excellent visual whenever there was a lull in play. He wanted alone time.

He wasn't going to question Glinda about her decision. She was a grown woman who knew what she wanted. He was glad it was him, and he'd make sure she didn't suffer for it while he was around. Workplace romances were perilous, but they paid off on occasion. And he was feeling lucky.

There was bound to be blowback. They'd hear about it on the set, from fans, from Fiona—although their shared agent's concerns would primarily be professional, since she made a point of staying out of her clients' private lives until it affected their work and her percentage.

Mike knew it was a risk, but everything was. He'd already dodged death twice since he and Glinda began working together. She'd suffered even worse luck than he did, and it hadn't deterred her. Her bravery was contagious.

So were her looks. The ones she'd been sneaking him as they inched toward their off-ramp were the sexiest things he'd ever seen. Forget pursed lips and the crossing and uncrossing of legs. Every time she raised one eyebrow a fraction of an inch, let the corners of her mouth quirk up a bit, and adjusted herself in the car's passenger seat, he got harder. Glinda was killing him, and enjoying every minute of it.

He was headed to his place. Her car was there. So was his California King mattress. He had a new, unopened box of condoms in his nightstand, so he was covered on that front. Mike grinned back at Glinda. It was a good thing they had time work out the kinks.

"Are we staying here?" she asked as they pulled into his garage.

"Unless you'd prefer we go to your place tonight?" He crossed his fingers that she didn't want to delay any further.

"No, I think I'd like to stay here."

She accepted his offer for a drink, and Mike toured her around his place. They strolled from the kitchen onto his patio, which overlooked the park and ball diamonds next door. He showed her his library in which he'd installed a full stereo system. It was his sanctuary that most visitors never got to see.

"How many bedrooms?" she asked as she set her glass beside the kitchen sink.

"Two."

"Why don't we check those out?"

"What happened to not rushing thing?"

"I gave you a whole extra day. Do you want longer?"

"Hell, no!"

She'd kicked her shoes off when they arrived and hooked her cap over one of the hooks at the front door. Now, as he led the way upstairs, she pulled her hair out of its ponytail. The curly locks exploded out of their confinement, surrounding her face like a halo. Her team shirt was already undone to the third button, giving hints of her cleavage without revealing anything. He stopped on the stairwell and gave it a tug, popping the next button. He stared down at her for moment, then laced his fingers through hers and doubled his pace.

Mike hadn't expected company that morning. He'd been in a rush to get their date started, but he had taken a moment to race around his bedroom tossing dirty clothes into the hamper and generally tidying up. That was all undone when Glinda tugged at his shirt hem. He helped her pull it over his head—she was too short—and threw it behind him to land where it may. Glenda peeled off her top, revealing a light pink bra that was more lace and bad intentions than substance.

She shimmied out of her jeans and let them pool around her feet for a second before she stepped out of them. Her underwear matched her bra. Just when he thought it wasn't possible for him to get harder, she had to prove him wrong.

He didn't need her help getting out of his pants. Her hands fumbling around his fly caused more problems than not. "Tease," he muttered. He picked her up under her arms and carefully dumped her onto the bed.

She scooted backwards, making room for him. "Are you going to keep me waiting, Mike?"

"Not a chance."

There was no reason to rush. He explored her, his fingertips brushing along all the soft, delicate places that were usually hidden. He trembled when she found a sensitive spot on the side of his ribcage.

"Are you ticklish or something?"

"Or something," he replied.

They'd touch for so long then return to each other for a kiss. He got hotter each time until he couldn't take it anymore.

"Where are you going?"

The tinfoil wrapper wrinkled in his hand. "Good thinking," Glinda said.

Unrolling the condom confirmed he didn't need any more foreplay. He was ready to go, but only if she was. He rolled over, taking her with him until she was flat on her back, and he was propped on his elbow, leaning over her. "Open up for me, beautiful."

He touched her knee, then slowly slid his hand between her thighs. Her legs parted, giving him enough room to place a knee between them. Her green eyes stared up at him, sending a shock straight down his spine. He bent to kiss her again. She pulled him against her chest, but he pushed himself back. "I'm too heavy."

"You're fine."

Mike nudged at her entrance. She was hot. Hot and so tight. Her sharp inhalation made him pause, but seeing the way she licked her lips made him keep going. He couldn't believe how good Glinda felt. He'd had her the night before, but it was like a foggy, long-ago dream he was remembering. This was so much more alive.

Her hips rolled, encouraging his to do the same. Her hands roamed up and down his arms and across his shoulders. He felt her fingers link at the base of his neck while she raised herself to meet him.

He tried to keep things slow, to prolong the exquisite sensations flowing through him, but his body wanted more. Faster. Harder. His tempo increased, and Glinda kept up with his pace.

"Oh. Mike. I'm." Glinda couldn't manage more than one word at a time. The pure need in her voice was intoxicating. Mike forced himself to stay exactly where he was until she was exactly where he wanted her to be.

"Come on, Glinda," he urged.

Then she did, clamping down on him, crying wordlessly. He held off until she finished and then let his control slip.

He collapsed beside her. He brushed a lock of hair off her face, where the sweat had pasted a curl to her cheek. "Wow. Thank you."

"Glinda, I cannot tell you enough how that was entirely my pleasure." It wasn't just the physical connection. The emotional one he felt while he caught his breath next to her was something he hadn't realized he'd missed so deeply when she hadn't been in his life.

"This is going to be fun," she said. "I hope you don't have plans to do anything else for a while."

Nope. Just her.

Chapter Twenty-One

Glinda was not limping. She wanted to, but she promised herself a long, hot bath if she made it into her house without thinking again of exactly what she'd done to earn her sore muscles.

Mike hadn't wanted her to go, but it was noon the day after the ballgame, and as much as she wanted to stay cocooned with him, she had to get home. There would be music to face.

Probably very loud, very annoying music.

She kept her phone turned off until she was chin deep in bubbles, the whirlpool function in her soaking tub whipping them into a delightful, lavender-scented froth. She scrolled through all her social media notifications, only bothering to pause if she recognized a name from somebody whose opinion mattered to her. There were more "Play ball!" comments than she could count. She responded to a dozen comments, then, after fortifying herself with a gulp of coffee, called up her voicemail.

It was full.

It wasn't surprising, but she made a point of keeping it empty. Anything with a blocked number was deleted first, bringing the total down to a still unreasonable but at least recognizable number of messages. Most could wait. Once couldn't.

"Hello, my favourite sister."

"I'm your only sister," Dory muttered.

"Whatever. Do you have a minute?"

"Or an hour," she said agreeably. "How was your date at the baseball game?"

"Why were you watching the Dodgers?" If Dory were watching anything, it would have been the Chicago Cubs with their dad.

"I wasn't. I have Google alerts on your name. My inbox was flooded with photos and links to the video."

"What did you think?"

"You looked good. And that was one hot kiss."

"Not helpful, Dory!"

"I don't know what you want me to say. I thought you had a policy about not dating your co-stars. In fact, we had a conversation before you started filming with him about 'oh, he's just a fellow actor toward whom I have no romantic intentions' Mike Mosley. Now he's got his tongue down your throat."

She wasn't wrong. Glinda got two big gulps of her coffee down before Dory spoke again. "Do you have anything to say for yourself?"

"I'm a big girl, and I'm allowed to change my mind. Nobody gets to choose who I date. Not even you, my favorite sister."

"Again, your only sister. But you're right. Are you going to be able to say the same thing to every reporter, producer, and director who asks you the same thing?

Because you're in the shit now, girlie. The gossips are going to love you."

"I'd better. I like him, Dory. A lot. He's intelligent and kind and—" He was everything she was looking for. He understood her in a way no other man had. She hadn't scared him off with her Pollyanna attitude, or the way she operated best by keeping half a dozen balls in the air to keep from getting bored. His stability to her bouncing around was comforting. His humor kept her on her toes. Every day, she looked forward to seeing him again. Mike was getting to be an addiction.

"Hot?"

"That too." Hot. Sizzling. Dazzlingly handsome on screen and twice as sexy close up.

"And black," her sister noted.

"Is that a problem?"

"Not with me. You do know we're a little homogenous back home, right?"

That was an understatement. Their high school ran the gamut of milk-white all the way to eggshell. There might have been one student who could have been considered light toast because he boasted a Greek grandmother who lived with them, but that was it.

"Should I expect some comments?"

"I don't mean to sound like a bitch, but you know they already talk about you here. This will just be a fresh reason. Am I going to meet Mr. Tall, Dark and Handsome any time soon?"

"Next time you're out," Glinda promised.

The rest of the conversation, and the cooling coffee, went much easier.

She slipped beneath the surface and held her breath, letting the bubbles and warm water surround her. Dorothy had done what Glinda wanted her to; eased her fears about her decision. She couldn't guarantee a successful future with Mike, but she could make sure they had the chance of one.

When the water was too cold to stay in the tub any longer, she crawled out and into a fresh set of clothes. She did her hair and makeup, and settled into her kitchen chair to make the call she'd left till last.

"Hi. It's Glinda Crawford for Fiona." As the receptionist put her through, Glinda pasted a smile on her face. She could do this.

"Glinda, that was a hell of an announcement. Your social media stats have gone through the roof. What are you planning for next time? And will you give me a heads-up?"

"Nope. My private life is my private life."

"I want to see you a week from today. Both of you," Fiona ordered.

"This isn't a negotiation," Glinda insisted.

"I'm pleased to see you standing up for yourself, cupcake, but this isn't about you. This is about work."

"Will we have a new script by then?" If they did, it was an insanely fast turnaround. Of course, an Academy award winning director probably had more than a few writers on speed dial.

"You will. Antonia's very excited and she's pushing hard on this rewrite. She'll tell you all about it. Show up at eight o'clock sharp. They want to resume filming as soon as possible."

If Antonia was excited, Glinda was too. "I'll be there," she promised. "With bells on."

Chapter Twenty-Two

Mike was glad he'd brought his own coffee. He needed the double espresso to steady his nerves. Glinda met his eyes across the table, and he smiled with encouragement. But not with much hope.

He smiled every time he was with her anyway. Even with all the shit they'd been through, Glinda had shown up ready to work, radiating cheerful vibes, and with no resentment about what she'd already been through on the production.

He'd been doing fine without Glinda in his life, but since they'd started this project, everything had gone just a little easier. Their physical attraction to each other hadn't been a surprise; he wasn't blind. Their compatibility on all other levels had been. He was falling hard. A few more days and there would be no coming back from what he felt for her.

His conversation the day before with Fiona about his future had been enlightening. When he'd started with *Olympus*, he'd been gearing down his acting career. He'd given his agent lots of notice about his intent. Signing on as a full cast member for *Olympus*, rather than a recurring role, had surprised her, but it had been his choice. If he were going to be around for a while longer now—and that was still a big *if* in his mind—he needed to change his attitude and start making plans.

By all indications, this movie was not going to help his longevity.

Antonia Caruso called the meeting to order, welcomed the third iteration of the production team, and introduced the quickly-hired new cast. Mike hadn't heard of most of them. He was shocked to see Rio Rodrigues at the table. His friend hadn't dropped a single hint. The tension in Mike's neck relaxed a little. Every steady hand they picked up would only make things easier. Rio was a one-take wonder, never flubbing a scene. With the production's latest schedule, they'd need every advantage they could get to finished on time.

Next, Antonia called out a trio of writers—Zubov, Ackerman, and Zano—who had lined the end of the table with laptops and pads of paper at their elbows. Glinda gave an excited peep. Their names rang a bell, but he was more interested in their product.

"Due to time constraints, we'll be keeping our writing team on hand for any changes that have to be made on the fly. It's rather exciting," Antonia said.

Mike had done his homework. The director had an image she'd maintained for more than two decades. She demanded and got the best. She ran her productions on time and on budget. And she always, always, took her work seriously. He didn't understand the mad gleam in her eye.

"We've decided to move away from action-adventure. It isn't my forte, and frankly, I have no interest in it. We've decided to switch to a genre that, in my opinion, has been languishing for some years," she continued.

Beside him, Glinda vibrated in anticipation. The more he got to know her, the more he realized how deeply her desire to be taken seriously ran. They'd talked about it. A breakout movie with Antonia Caruso was so far beyond the scope of possibility it had never come up.

"Are you leaning more toward *April, May and June*, or *The Bell*?" Glinda asked. The two movies in question were Antonia's first film, a multi-generational family saga, and her latest, a post-war drama.

"This is like nothing I've ever done before. You will be breaking new ground with me."

Suddenly, Mike knew. He knew exactly where Antonia was headed, and he didn't like it one bit. It wouldn't hurt him, but Glinda was going to be devastated.

"Comedy. Broad, physical comedy with puns and straight men and outrageous situations with even zanier outcomes. Bro comedies have their place, but I want to return to the classics."

He was surprised Glinda was more excited than ever. "Define classic," she ordered.

"*Airplane* and *Bringing Up Baby* and a touch of the cult classics."

Antonia's announcement stunned the room into silence.

"Let's see it," Glinda said.

Antonia crooked her finger at a P.A. in the corner. The whip-thin assistant began dropping scripts in front of everyone around the table.

"Pandemonium?" Mike asked.

"No. Pan-*da*. *Panda-monium*," she corrected.

God, it sounded worse than he imagined.

Glinda took a deep breath and flipped the cover open.

He did the same.

The first page wasn't horrible. His character was still named Dr. Monty Hanzel, and he was still a veterinarian, but this time he was a veterinary engineer, whatever that was. The film started with him training some dogs in his laboratory. So far, he could work with it.

On the second page, army captain Jane Mackenzie arrived in her Lamborghini, and Mike's heart dropped. Jane told Monty his work on cybernetic implants for military guard dogs been stolen by a foreign arms dealer, and had been adapted for other animals. However, said arms dealer was having difficulty making the final modifications work and was planning to kidnap the inventor so Monty could fix them. Jane was there to protect him until the arms dealer was caught.

On page four, the duo was attacked by a squad of Chinese ninjas outside Monty's lab.

"Chinese ninjas?" Mike said in disbelief.

"Is there a problem?" one of the writers asked. Mike thought it might be Ackerman.

"Ninjas are Japanese."

"These guys aren't ninjas, per se. They are specially trained warriors. Later we discover they are loyal to a Chinese warlord who runs a terrorist cell, so they're more like samurai."

"Also Japanese," Mike protested.

One of the Z-writers raised his hand. "Hold on. That's good, let me get it down."

"Why?"

"We might be able to use it later," the screenwriter said.

By the time they'd finished their exchange, Glinda was a few pages ahead of him and hooting in laughter. "He ends up naked. Excellent!"

"Who? Me?" He wasn't doing nude scenes. Glinda knew that. Of course, it was a bit of a compliment that she wanted to see him naked again. He felt the same way, but he'd prefer the privacy of his bedroom. Or hers. Looking at the spark in her eye and the pure, unadulterated joy in her smile, he wanted it sooner rather than later.

"No, the Chinese ninja samurai. I Kung-Fu his clothes off."

Mike groaned.

"What now?"

"Kung-Fu *is* Chinese."

"Oh, he's perfect," Antonia said.

"Don't I know it," Glinda agreed with a grin.

Mike didn't understand the looks flying between the women.

But he feared them.

Chapter Twenty-Three

It wasn't what she'd asked for, but she wasn't heartbroken. From the beginning, Glinda had dreamed of a dramatic role. Something new that would allow her to stretch professionally. It was why she signed on. Comedy was a different beast. She was good at it, and she knew it, but it wasn't what she'd planned on doing.

As ridiculous as the script was, part of her was excited for *Panda-monium*. She wasn't crazy, although she wouldn't blame anyone for thinking she was after the first two attempts to get the production off the ground. Glinda trusted Antonia Caruso. How could she not, when the director had begun by hiring three of the top-rated comedy writers in the business? Zubov, the oldest of the trio by twenty years, hadn't released a movie in the last decade, but he'd dominated the box office in the nineties and the first couple years of the millennium. Ackerman had brought back-to-back hits to her studio, and Zano was a renowned script doctor. If this was the last chance to save the production, Antonia had brought her A-game.

Mike, on the other hand, did not see any of that. He saw bad writing instead of satire, and no way for the production to recover from two strikes. Glinda sighed and put an extra bottle of beer in the fridge. Mike had already had several solid, dramatic roles. He'd never been the comic relief. What confused her was why he was so concerned. From what he'd said, this was his swan song.

She read the script again in the waiting room of her doctor's office. It was her final post-Hawaiian disaster checkup before she was certified fully recovered. She fought a yawn while she waited. Mike had eaten into a lot of her sleep time lately. She wasn't complaining, but a girl could not live on orgasms alone.

The disposable blue gown did little to protect Glinda from the cold vinyl examination table. She'd finally found a position where none of her exposed skin was in direct contact with the cold plastic when Dr. Constance Booth limped into the exam room.

"What's wrong with you?" Glinda asked.

"You are such an actress. Quit stealing my lines." Connie Booth was a second-generation Barrow Jackson doctor. When Glinda first moved to Los Angeles, she'd found a female doctor who was old enough to be her grandmother, but spry enough to make Glinda look bad. One of the clinic's original founders, Doctor Barrow lived and breathed yoga as part of a balanced life, prescribed fruit and nut granola with Greek yogurt for regularity, and a good steak and dry martini when her patients felt overwhelmed and needed to regroup for the next battle.

Glinda had been devastated when she'd retired to Arizona. Doctor Barrow had passed the baton, and her patient list, to Dr. Constance Booth. She was smart, intuitive, and took pride in communication with her patients. When she was in the room with one, all her attention was in the room. Connie had never brushed off any of Glinda's concerns, from adjusting the dosage of her anti-anxiety meds, to the allergy to mussels she'd developed out of nowhere.

Originally, Glinda wasn't thrilled about having a doctor who was younger than she was, but there were some benefits. Like the fact that Connie still remembered what it was like to work stupid, crazy hours for a job you loved, and that quitting wasn't an option.

"Seriously, what happened?" Glinda asked.

"I twisted my ankle kicking another doctor's ass at the Riverside Clinic. He tried to brush off appendicitis as menstrual cramps. On a ten-year-old."

"I hope that kick was literal."

"It's the only way to get through to assholes," Connie punned. She smirked, and reminded Glinda yet again of how young she was. "But enough about me. What brings you in today?"

"Exhaustion beyond normal. I'm sleeping and eating, and I can't shake it. I promised my sister I'd come in because she's concerned I picked up something in Hawaii."

"We can look. Sex?"

"Had some lately. I'm good," Glinda joked.

"Protection?"

"I'm on the pill and haven't missed any, and he uses condoms. I'm not nauseous, my boobs aren't sore, and my period is still like clockwork."

Dr. Booth nodded. She was the one who'd prescribed the new birth control after changes in Glinda's old one made her acne flare up. "Okay. I'm going run a full panel anyway. How about the other usual suspects? Multi-vitamins?"

"Yes."

"Vitamin D?"

Even living in California, Glinda couldn't get enough sunshine. Her complexion couldn't handle the sun. "Chewable vitamin D and calcium gummies."

"Iron?"

Glinda paused. She sorted her vitamins into a container every Sunday morning. She was ninety per cent sure there hadn't been a red pill for the last week. She specifically remembered empting the bottle when she filled the little squares for her trip to Hawaii, then tossing the empty bottle into recycling. But she'd opened a new one when she'd returned home and put it with her other vitamins, hadn't she?

"Iron?" Connie repeated.

"Shit."

"Have you been crunching ice?"

She had been, but she hadn't thought about it. The SoCal temperatures had been higher than normal and she was making an effort to stay hydrated.

"Shit," Glinda repeated.

"Pick some up today. Double up to a thousand milligrams for the next week, then drop down to your regular five hundred. You can't afford to become anemic, so help yourself. You're smarter than this."

Glinda took the lecture without a word of complaint because she deserved it. Running out of iron was a rookie mistake, and she'd been dealing with her low blood iron for years. It was fixable, and experience had taught her she'd bounce back fast enough that the drag-ass feeling that had been plaguing her would be gone in a week. Iron pills, red meat, green veggies and faking it for a few days until it all kicked it. She could do that. "Thanks, doc."

"Oh, no, you're still getting the panel," Constance insisted. "I need to know how low your numbers are." She scrawled something on a lab order and handed it to Glinda. "Stop at the lab on your way out. They'll fit you in."

Glinda hated needles, hated feeling stupid, and she was sick and tired of being sick and tired. She dutifully headed to the lab, and bit back a snarky comment when the lab tech stuck her with a needle. She even laughed when the tech gave her a lollipop for not crying. She hadn't smiled bravely for the candy; she'd done it out of fear she'd get a bigger needle next time.

Chapter Twenty-Four

She had enough time to pick up her new prescription and two thick steaks, and still make it home in time to prepare for her date. She'd changed into leggings and a fitted silk shirt over a tank top. She wanted something sexy and casual, but more importantly, something she could move in. They would begin starting as soon as Antonia got all her ducks in a row, which meant it could be the last evening they had off at the same time for a while. Glinda didn't want to waste any time getting stuck in her clothes.

She saw Mike's hands, and some of his forearms. The rest of him, including his head, was hidden behind a massive bouquet of white and red roses.

"Oh, wow, gorgeous!"

He shifted the flowers, and she was gratified to see her response was the right one. But there were still stress lines pulling at the corners of his eyes, and his smile was not as broad as it could be, so she went for the laugh. "The flowers aren't bad either." The lines receded and she knew her joke had hit its mark. "Come on in."

She got a quick peck when he handed over the bouquet. As soon as she'd clipped the stems and dropped them into a crystal vase, he swooped in again. He lips pressed against hers harder than they had at their kiss goodbye the night before. His hands were more frantic as they roamed across her back and pulled her tight against him.

As heat bloomed in her core, she braced her hands on the edge of the cupboard and hopped onto the countertop. From that height, she could wrap her legs around his waist and grind herself against him. They had a lot to talk about regarding work, but that could be done over dinner.

Glinda wanted dessert first.

She knew about his sensitive ears, but when she exhaled and her warm breath hit his collarbone, Mike shivered all over. "Good spot?" she asked.

"Very good."

"How about this one?" She lifted her hips and ground herself against the fly of his jeans.

"Also good. Where's the bed?"

He carried her down the hall while she searched for other places that made him catch his breath. There was a spot at the base of his ribs, a line across his hipbone, and everything south of that.

He found a few of her secret places too. The skin under the curve of her breast, the small of her back. There was no hurry to find all the ways they could make each other gasp and moan. By the time she offered him a condom from her nightstand, she couldn't keep her hands off him if she wanted, and so she didn't try. He took her mouth with his as he eased himself into her. Then he stroked her with gentle, firm strokes until she lost control.

"I like that. I like what you sound like when you do that. Let's do it again," Mike said. Then he kept his promise, taking her there again before joining her.

Her head was spinning, but her body was exhausted. She ached in all the best places. Glinda faked a shiver when Mike lifted the covers to rejoin her in bed. She'd already packed pillows against the headboard so they could sit up and talk.

"We definitely need more meeting days," he said.

"Not arguing."

He tugged at her until she fell on his chest. "Antonia turned it into a comedy. I didn't expect our meeting to go like that. Did you?"

"I want to say no, but the option was at the back of my mind," she admitted.

"It was?"

"It was the easy play. Action-adventure means stunts and explosions and special effects, and the budget is already blown. The studio could have returned us to the original script, or a variation thereof, but with the publicity it has already received as a drama, it would be hard to overcome the bad impression the public already has about it. I'm not saying comedy is easy, but it can be cheap."

"You wanted to do a serious drama. To, how did you put it? '...show them you aren't a joke.' Now you're stuck doing jokes," he said. His voice was soft and kind, as was the hug he gave her when he said it.

Glinda snuggled deeper into his arms, revelling in the comfort he was offering. "I was, and I did. But I've been thinking—is it such a bad thing to make people laugh? A dramatic role isn't going to change what strangers think when they look at me. And in this town, a hit is a hit."

"But it's not what you wanted," he pressed.

"It's like wanting a Bentley and ending up with a Mercedes. It's not the same, but are you really going to bitch about a free luxury car?"

"Glinda. You had your heart set on a drama."

"I had my heart set on people taking me seriously. And they will. This is a different route to the same destination."

Mike squeezed her again. "It's not what I wanted for you. I want you to have everything. I want to be the one who makes sure you are happy."

She kissed him for that. "Thank you. It is what it is, and it could have been much, much worse. Plus, I wouldn't have you if it weren't for *Panda-monium*, so, overall, I'm counting it as a win. I like having you."

"It did bring us together." He rolled over, bringing her with him. Her knees straddled his waist, and she crossed her arms on his chest so she could look down on him. The sheet slid down her back, drawing a shiver as the cool air hit her skin. "Are you really okay with it?"

She shrugged, purposefully, to let the sheet slip lower. "Our luck has been pretty volatile. I'll take the good while I can."

"Good plan."

She wiggled, then laughed at his groan. "What do you say—do you want to get lucky?"

Chapter Twenty-Five

Mike stared at the paper he'd taped to the bathroom mirror. It was a copy of his medical results from the physical he'd taken before the start of production, and the numbers weren't pretty. It said he had the cholesterol levels of a man almost ten years older. His blood pressure was high, too, but still below the level where he'd need medication. Thankfully his BMI index was lower than average, but his workouts were a decision he made for his bank account, not his health. He had to do better.

The letter shocked the hell out of him. If was going to stay in the business, he couldn't afford to slack off anymore. Even worse, he had lost ground to make up. He could defer it until after he was finished filming, but that would only put him further behind the eight ball. It was time to swallow his pride and work toward his future.

He reached for his phone, deciding his mother's brother was his best place to start. "Hey, Uncle Micah, how's retirement going?" After forty years, his uncle had sold his furniture store and retired with a paid-for house and a membership to a public golf course.

"I double-bogeyed three holes in a row yesterday. I'm going back to work. It's less stressful," the old man complained.

"Can I hit you up for some advice before you tee off this morning?"

"What's up?"

Mike knew his uncle had no patience with delicacy or beating around the bush. Still, he spent a few seconds coming up with a softer way to ask what changes Micah had made to his diet and lifestyle after a heart attack had almost taken him out at fifty. "Remember when your doctor gave you a list of things to reduce your chance of heart attack, and you bitched about it for two months while Aunt Jen tried to get you to cut back on fried food and start eating more natural fiber? I need that list."

"What's wrong? Did something happen? Are you in the hospital?"

"I'm fine, but it has recently come to my attention that fried eggs and sausage for breakfast everyday has consequences once you pass thirty. I'm looking for preventative measures. Do you still have that list?"

"Give me a minute." had listened to his uncle's footsteps cross a tile floor.

"Are you wearing your golf shoes inside the house? Aunt Jen is going to kill you!"

"I was practicing my putting in the yard, and she's at the store buying green crap. Who's going to tell her? You, Mr. I Need a Favor?"

"No, sir."

"I'm going to take some pictures and send them to you. Good enough?"

"Thanks, Uncle Micah."

Mike hadn't looked at them yet, aside to check that they were legible. He hit the next name on his mental list while he surveyed the contents of his fridge. A lot of it needed to go. He shouldn't be keeping bacon in his vegetable crisper anyway. "Hey, buddy, how's things?"

"We're just back from San Diego Comic Con. Ashleigh tagged along for a couple days, and now she's down with con crud, so I'm looking after her. Why? What's up?" Nick Thurston asked.

Prior to Glinda, Mike would have thought it was cute that Nick was taking care of his dance instructor sweetheart. After watching his girlfriend bounce around a gully and, later, Johnny Chung's stage, he understood why Nick wanted to keep an eye on his girlfriend. "You know that trainer you're always raving-slash-complaining about? Is he taking new clients?"

"Trey? I don't know. Do you want me to call him?"

"Please. If he is, give him my number, and we'll set something up."

The silence on the line drew out so long Mike thought they'd been disconnected. "Nick, are you still there?"

"I'm here. Are you sure you want to do this? Trey will get the job done, don't get me wrong, but there are less intense trainers out there who might be a better fit for you."

"Don't worry. I'll be fine."

HE WAS NOT FINE.

At the moment, it was all Mike could do to not hunt down Nick and kill him for introducing him to Satan. Trey Donavan believed in two speeds: fast, and overdrive. They'd had an initial appointment and two sessions in the last six days.

Mike would have rebelled if he had the energy.

Now he was on set with Rio, filming a scene where the vet and the pilot were escaping with the MacGuffin after their army bodyguard sacrificed herself to ensure their successful getaway. For the moment, they were strapped into a mock helicopter waiting for their mic packs to be replaced.

"What's wrong with you? You've been dragging ass for days," Rio said. "Are you turning into an old man or what?"

"Fuck off. Do you know Trey Donavan?"

He didn't expect the bark of laughter he got in response to his question. "You poor bastard. Why did you go and do a thing like that?"

"Because young guns like you are sneaking up behind me, and I need to be able to fight you off for the good parts."

"What session are you on?"

"I had my second yesterday," Mike complained.

"It gets easier once you hit double digits. Then you really start to notice the difference. But until then, I'd invest in muscle liniment stock." The bastard laughed at him again. "Seriously, though, are you doing okay? Heavy comedy is way out of your wheelhouse."

"They knew what they were getting coming in. I'm fine. You know what's funny? Ferris Lorde bitched about Glinda's lack of professionalism when this was a drama. Robert Roth too, although he was all about getting her naked. She's the one they were bitching about settling for."

"Shit, that's harsh."

"I know. She's the only reason we got as much usable footage as we did. She was an absolute queen on the set, keeping the crews together. I'm afraid I'm the one who is going to be the weak link."

"Nobody has any complaints yet. You keep setting them up, and Glinda will keep knocking them down. That is one funny woman."

"Damned straight."

Rio laughed at him again. "You've got it bad, my friend."

"You're not kidding." Mike hadn't thought it was possible to fall harder for her, but here he was. He even thought her acting was perfect.

He was the straight man to her jokes, and she nailed each and every one of them. The hardest part was not laughing at her delivery. Nearly every page had a punchline: from the Chinese ninjas on the second page to Captain Mackenzie's Army Ranger career with a joint PhDs in Computer Sciences and Artificial Intelligence and a fluency in Chinese and Russian, to his ability to Dr. Doolittle every animal they came across. Absolutely everything was fair game and over the top.

Yet, the script wasn't stupid. Or thoughtless. There was no mistaking it for highbrow, but the audience would have to pay attention to catch all the jokes. He'd love to sit in the back of the theater to people-watch.

Or better yet, take Glinda to a showing and let her steal all his popcorn while he stole kisses.

The sooner they finished this movie, the better.

Chapter Twenty-Six

"You know what's funny? Ferris Lorde bitched about Glinda's lack of professionalism when this was a drama. Robert Roth too, although he was all about getting her naked. She's the one they were bitching about settling for."

She's the one they settled for.

Settled for.

Glinda couldn't drown out Mike's words, no matter how loud she cranked the car stereo.

She'd come to the studio on her day off to surprise him. There was a surprise alright.

Settled for.

She hadn't even been eavesdropping. She'd walked up, plain as day. Two of the grips had called out greetings to her. The only *good* surprise was that nobody else had been close enough to hear him.

It didn't matter. Mike was a much better actor than she was. He'd had her convinced he took her seriously as an actress. He'd gone to a lot of work to make her believe it and get into her pants. He must have thought it was hilarious when she threw herself at him the very next day.

She was going to end up tabloid fodder after all.

Glinda stayed in control until she crossed the threshold and then collapsed in her foyer. Tears scalded her cheeks. The worst part was that she couldn't even call her sister; Dorothy had warned her about fishing in the work dating pool.

Glinda crawled back under the covers. Her stomach was a mess, but the thought of putting anything in it only made her feel worse.

Settled for.

She pushed that part of the conversation aside and concentrated on the rest, replaying the whole scene in her mind. Nobody else appeared to have heard Mike's comments; if he and Rio kept the conversation to themselves, she only had to fake it in front of the two of them for the duration of filming. At least she knew why Mike hadn't made the effort to find time to see her. If he couldn't get her in bed, she wasn't worth his time.

She didn't have the energy to answer the phone, but she checked her voicemail afterwards. Dr. Booth wanted to redo some of the tests. She'd made an appointment at the lab for Glinda's convenience since they didn't need to meet in person. It looked like she'd be getting that iron shot after all.

Glinda dragged her purse onto the bed and checked the most recent call sheet. She and Mike were scheduled to work together the next day. She had twelve hours to hit the lab and pull herself together.

She thought she did a good job. If Mike noticed her cold shoulder, he wasn't saying anything. As if the tension between them wasn't enough, he was messing with everyone else as well. After he flubbed his lines for the third time in a row, Antonia called a halt to filming.

"Mike, take a couple minutes and regroup," Antonia said. "Everyone else, reset."

"Are you okay?" Glinda asked as the set cleared.

"Fine."

"Do you want to run the scene quickly?"

"I know my lines. I want you to not hover," he snapped.

"Can do. Get it fucking right next time." She'd covered her microphone again, for both their sakes, but if he wasn't going to pretend to care anymore, he didn't deserve anything more than the most basic courtesy of her not humiliating him in front of the crew.

When Antonia called them back to action, Glinda was back in place with her smile firmly fixed, and the same warm glow in her eyes she'd had during the last take. She didn't give him the courtesy of a shitty look to tell him she was still pissed. It was like what he'd done to her and what they had didn't even register. Mike finally got his lines right, but as soon as they cut, Glinda was off again, to a scene that didn't need him.

She didn't look back. If he wanted her to be more professional, she'd cut everything non-work related on set.

Starting with him.

Chapter Twenty-Seven

Mike wasn't proud of himself, but it had to be done. He needed something to make him smile. He and Nick had been comparing notes on Trey's workout regimes, and Nick had let it slip that the diet portion of his program was killing him. Mike sent him a combination thanks for the introduction/good luck with the diet present.

Five pounds of assorted candies and chocolates, and five dozen donuts.

Payback was going to be a bitch, but today it made him feel better.

He'd take any relief he could get. Something was off with Glinda and he had no idea what it was. She avoided him, dodged his calls, and when they weren't working together, if the cameras weren't running, she froze him out. He didn't get it. He had something he needed to discuss with her and she was making it next to impossible.

Thank God for friends who knocked some sense into him.

"What the fuck is wrong with you, Mike? If you're hurting from your training sessions, you take a fucking painkiller and you do the job," Rio growled, his dark eyes sparking.

"What?"

"So far this morning, you've bitched out the craft services people for handing you a wet water bottle, yelled at wardrobe because your boots pinched, and thrown a fit because you almost got a splinter."

"I did not."

Rio stared him down. Mike knew he'd been a little irritable but he hadn't been that bad.

A trembling young woman approached him with a towel. She finished wiping a water bottle and handed it to him. "Here you go, Mr. Mosley. It's dry."

Except evidently, he had been. "Thanks a lot. I appreciate it."

She sighed as she left, like she'd escaped execution. "What else?" Mike asked Rio.

"You should probably apologize to everyone for being an asshole. Twice to me, and three times to Glinda. She flubbed her lines once this morning and you nearly took her head off. Do you know how often you've screwed up in the last week?"

It had been more often than he liked. Looking back, Glinda had been as patient as ever until he'd snapped. Then she'd disappeared before he had a chance to apologize. He kept meaning to get around to it, but something always came up. He hadn't realized how much her absence had weighed on him until he thought about it. "Sorry I've been such a dick. You're right, I'll take something and suck up my complaints."

Rio smiled. "No worries, Mike. I know how grumpy older guys can get."

"Get off my lawn!"

It took most of the morning to soothe all the feathers he'd ruffled. He'd spread his bad mood far and wide. Rio's verbal slap had cleared his head fog. His body would get used to his workouts, but nobody else had to suffer through them.

Glinda was hiding from him again. Now he understood why. He spotted her going into her trailer, and chased after her. A P.A. was heading in her direction, so he relieved him of his delivery and knocked on Glinda's door instead.

"Hi…hey," she said, when she saw it wasn't who she was expecting.

"I wish I had time to get flowers to go with this apology. I'm sorry I've been acting like such an asshole, and I'm doubly sorry for taking my foul mood out on you." The distance in her eyes made him doubt his words would be enough.

She crossed her arms, blocking any chance he had to grovel out of the public eye. "Oh? Tell me more."

"I started with a new personal trainer last week—"

"In the middle of filming?" she interrupted.

"Yes, which makes me an idiot, I know. He's been kicking my ass, and even though it's self-inflicted I've been taking it out on everyone around me. Since you've been the closest, you've been getting the brunt of it. I didn't know how much until today. I'm sorry, Glinda. It's bad enough we haven't had any time together in the last week, but I've been making the little time we did have uncomfortable for you. My mouth is the only part of me not affected and I ran it off. I'm sorry."

He saw her thaw a little, which made him feel even worse. Glinda was low drama. If he'd wound her up so much that his physical presence made her tense, one apology wasn't going to cut it. "According to our schedules, we're both off tomorrow. Can I see you to apologize properly? I can make us lunch at my place. I miss you."

It took forever for her to give a small nod of agreement. "You do?"

"Of course, I do. I need my Glinda fix."

He thought that would earn him a smile, but he evidently wasn't forgiven. He could tell by the set of her shoulders and the tightness to her voice. But she said, "I guess we can talk."

It wasn't a great beginning, but it was a start.

Work still wasn't a lot of fun. His body hurt, his head ached from the constant battle to bite his tongue when he was being unreasonable, and the hours seemed even longer than usual.

He saw Trey the next morning since he was off, and the workout wasn't as horrible as it had been. The trainer left, giving Mike enough time to shower before Glinda arrived for the lunch he'd planned for them.

Mike had brought girls home before. Never seriously. There were always holiday parties and football, rib, and wing nights. This lunch was for the express purpose of getting Glinda and his family together, and he was having second thoughts. He hadn't meant to spring it on her like he was now doing, but he didn't want to wait. He could apologize in private first, and then make the introductions.

There was no doubt he was in love with her. Like, for the rest of his days, she was the one love. But he hadn't told her yet. Today was the day. He'd wasted enough time, and almost blown his shot in the meantime. He refused to risk things again.

She had to know it was coming. He knew her. She'd said before—not to him, but he'd heard her say it—that she was looking for something serious. They may not have begun that way, but they'd got there in a hurry. They both knew it. They were good together. Why should they wait?

The restaurant delivery was due in an hour, and he'd invited his dad, aunt, and uncle to come over an hour after that.

So, of course, they arrived before the food.

His aunt and uncle brought flowers. "Just unwrap the bottom and stick them in a vase for now," Uncle Micah ordered.

"You don't want me to open them?"

"They aren't for you." The old man grinned. "We're happy for you, Mike."

He hadn't told them why he'd invited them to lunch. He hadn't even thought it in their general direction out of fear they might pick up on what he intended to do.

"I can't wait to meet her," his aunt Jen said, "although I've got a pretty good sense of what she's like. She's a pretty little doll on *Olympus*. But these last few weeks, in the news, and saving your behind? I already like her a lot. You need someone who can keep an eye on you."

"I am not having this conversation with you right now," Mike protested. Possibly later. Preferably never.

"Your mom would be thrilled."

"Uncle Micah, please stop. Please."

The man he was named after did stop talking. But he raised his hand and lay his palm on Mike's face. "It's about time you settled."

Then Trent and Vanessa Vaughn showed up out of nowhere, bearing beer and pretzels. Vanessa took one look at the half-opened flowers on the dining room table, and the tin-foil containers stacked beside them, and froze in the doorway. "Do we have the wrong day?"

"For what?"

"Australian finals?"

Mike's head dropped. He'd promised to host the crew to a volleyball championship barbecue weeks ago, long before shooting began. That also meant Sean Glenn was on his way, and he'd asked if he could bring his girlfriend.

"We should go," Vanessa said to her brother before he could answer. "Mike's obviously got something else going today. We can watch at my place," she offered.

"What?" Trent protested. "Mike didn't forget. He—" Vanessa put a hand on his stomach, then pinched it violently. "Ow, dammit, Vanessa. Fine, your place." Trent rubbed his chest, his curled fingers catching on the material. "But he still owes us wings."

"Next time," Mike said thankfully.

"Can you text Rio our number?"

Mike saw Vanessa's shoulders stiffen at the request, but he didn't have time to wonder what his friend had done to garner that kind of reaction "Will do."

He'd barely got them out the door and returned to the kitchen when his doorbell rang again.

At least everyone was on the patio. He had some time to ease Glinda into his surprise. "Hello, gorgeous." He tossed her purse onto the dining room table, and pulled her into his arms.

The feel of his arms around her brought home how right he was to move now. If he'd waited much longer it would have been too late to do everything he wanted to do with her.

"I said we needed to talk." He felt his heart pounding in his chest, beating against his ribcage like it was trying to escape. Mike fingered the velvet box in his pocket. "We've been working really hard. We haven't had any time lately."

She nodded, her eyes serious. "I know. Can we do that now? I heard what you said to Rio the other day. About what Lorde and Roth said about me," she began.

It took him a moment to recall that conversation. "I meant every word."

Chapter Twenty-Eight

The man had balls. Glinda expected lies. Prevarication at the very least. A welcoming hug and confessing to her face left her speechless. For a minute.

"You did?" she asked. She took a step back, stiffening her spine and raising her chin. He was not going to beat her down.

"Glinda?"

"What?" Did he expect hugs and kisses after his admission?

The grating sound of metal on metal tore through the room. A sliding door opened and a strange man barreled into the room. "Mike, we need more ice why hello there!" he said, blending sentences in one breath. He was shorter than Mike, and heavier, but Glinda wouldn't be able to mistake him for anyone but family. "So, you're Mike's new girl. I've seen you on *Olympus*."

"Dad, ice is in the kitchen. I need to finish talking to Glinda and we'll be right out."

The older man nodded. "You take your time. I know settling can be hard to accept sometimes. Nice to meet you, Glinda."

Her heart sank but she gave his father her best fan smile. "You, too. Thanks for watching," she said.

"That was rude, don't you think?"

"As opposed to your father calling me your consolation girlfriend?"

"What? He did not."

"What is wrong with you? You just told me the same thing."

"What are you talking about?"

He was looking at her like she was insane, and her last thread of control snapped. She couldn't force him not to insult her, but she could call him on his lies. "The first time you called me second rate I thought it was a mistake. Now I know it wasn't."

"I never—"

"Our first date at the restaurant when you said it was time you settled because you were getting older? Ring a bell? Because I sure as hell remember, especially when your dad comes in and says I'm not what he wanted for you, but I'll do."

"Glinda, you know that's not what either of us meant. It's an expression."

"Oh? What exactly were you expressing when you told Rio that it was funny how Roth and Lorde both bitched about settling for me as an actress?"

She saw the wheels turning behind his eyes, but no lightbulb appeared over his head. It was like he was so used to trash-talking her he couldn't remember a single conversation. When his eyebrows slowly began to rise, she cut him off before he could offer yet another excuse. "Yeah, that. You know what, Mike? You got lucky. You don't need to settle anymore." Glinda leaned in close. "And neither do I."

She whirled on her heel and went straight out the door. She didn't slam it, nor did she make a point of ensuring his father saw her flounce away. Mike could explain.

Her strength petered out four blocks from his house. Glinda pulled to the curb while she could still see. She didn't yell or beat the steering wheel, but she couldn't stop the tears.

She didn't try. She held a tissue to her eyes, covered her face, and let them come. Her cheeks burned under the flow; humiliation hurt. The emotional storm didn't last long. She hoped she'd been subtle enough to not garner any attention.

In the time it took her to get home, she'd already replayed the scene in her head three times, improving it in each version until Mike knew exactly how big an ass he'd been, and how much his life was going to suck without her in it.

It didn't make the pit in her stomach feel any better, or plug the hole in her heart. What she needed was absolute sympathy and a shoulder to cry on. She knew where to find that, so she did what she always did and pulled out her phone.

"Hey, my favourite sister," she said, sniffling by the time she finished her greeting.

The noise on the other end of the line faded, and Glinda heard the click of a door being closed. "You sound terrible. What happened?"

Then the tears started again.

Chapter Twenty-Nine

He wanted to take it back. All of it, starting with dinner with Fiona at the Limelight. *The Bamboo Mountain*, *Extinction Level Event*, *Panda-monium*: whatever they wanted to call it, it sucked. He hadn't thought things could get worse, but here he was.

He still had no idea what had happened at his place the day before. Everything had been going fine, and then they were over. No warning. No explanation. Glinda was irate at something he'd supposedly done, and he'd returned the feeling with how she'd treated his family.

The burning humiliation of explaining to his father where his girlfriend went had faded, but his desire for enlightenment hadn't.

Part of him wanted to track her down and demand an answer. Another part wanted her to come to him to apologize, since he hadn't done a single thing wrong. A third part wanted to hurt her as badly as she'd hurt him, and a fourth part whispered to forget they'd ever had anything at all, and to act like strangers who had to work together.

God knew Glinda had that one down pat. He knew her inside out, but unless the cameras were rolling, there was a distance in her eyes that couldn't be measured in anything smaller than light years.

He was alternating between two and four. They'd been good together, very good, but they'd burned out. Or fizzled. Either way, they hadn't been together long enough for him to feel what they'd felt for each other, what he thought they'd felt. Evidently, it hadn't been real. It had simply carried over from the job. It wasn't the first time it had happened, and it wouldn't be the last. Once the dust settled, they'd find their new normal and go their separate ways. It sucked right now, but he'd learn to live with it.

Even with his new attitude, he was struggling. There were no words for the insanity *Panda-monium* had become in the last couple days.

There was a whiff of desperation on the set. Scene changes were more rushed than usual, and the pressure to get it all right on the first take was evident. But that was normal production stress, not the toxic brew the crew had been drowning in with their first two directors. Thankfully, the tension between him and Glinda was buried so deep nobody else had noticed it yet.

He took his cue from her and hid in his trailer when he wasn't needed. It didn't give anyone a chance to ask questions, and with the amount of script changes coming at him every day, nobody would question his need to be alone.

An unexpected knock on his door brought him to his feet.

If he'd known it was Robert Roth, he wouldn't have bothered. "Can I help you?"

"We need to talk."

Robert had badly overplayed his hand with the panda incident, but it didn't mean he was permanently out of the industry. If Mike wanted to keep working, he couldn't afford to slam the door in his face no matter how much the director deserved it.

"This is fine. I have to head back to the set in a minute," Mike lied.

"Mistakes were made with *Extinction Level Event*. Mistakes that weren't my fault, although I take responsibility for my reaction to them."

So, he wasn't trying to talk Mike out of a lawsuit for the panda-strangling, but he did want something. Mike nodded to let him continue. He knew Roth would hang himself if he had enough rope.

"Antonia Caruso is a fairly talented director, but she has no idea how to do anything but European dramas. Her version of a comedy won't play to American audiences. I've heard a dozen stories coming off the set about this disaster in the making. I think I can save it, if I can take the fact you're with me to the producers."

"They aren't going to hand the reins back to you. Not now. They'll kill the project before they make any more changes."

Roth nodded. "It's a possibility. But it would help if you were with me when I made the offer. It will look good on my next project. I have the script lined up, a feature, and I need to know I can work with the lead. That could be you, Mike."

Robert Roth had on a downward slide before he'd picked up the second unit director position; that was undeniable. It didn't mean he was untalented; he'd simply been overshadowed by all the new kids on the block. *Extinction Level Event* got people talking about him again, and, in the end, the industry was built on buzz. Mike didn't like Roth, but it didn't mean the other man was full of shit. Having a new project on the table before *Panda-monium* finished would kick his career back into high gear.

"I know we didn't get off to the best start, but that's not our fault. Glinda Crawford is a walking catastrophe. I can't imagine how hard it must be for you to do comedy with her. She didn't have the chops for action, and that was mostly her standing around with her tits out. This must be infinitely worse," Roth continued.

Glinda, his girlfriend, was gone. If she weren't, he would have flattened Roth for speaking about her like she was disposable piece of ass. He knew what it said about Roth that he didn't hesitate to do it. To the director, all women were.

But Glinda-the-actress was still his co-worker, here and on *Olympus*. And, professionally, he owed her his loyalty. No matter what had happened between them, he never doubted that she'd have his back in a similar situation. "We're done here."

"What?"

"Glinda Crawford is an excellent actress and an even better person. We're lucky to have her."

"Look, I know you're fucking her—"

"Stop. Seriously," Mike warned. "I've got twenty years of experience on her, and I'm telling you she's the reason the wheels haven't fallen off this production. She's quick, competent, and she can adapt to any asshole she's forced to work with." He didn't elaborate, but Roth was quick to pick up the insult.

"You should really reconsider your decision. This business changes fast. You never know who you're going to need a favor from."

Roth missed the irony of his statement, since he'd shown up at Mike's door for that exact reason. "My career will survive," he deadpanned.

Roth postured and huffed, but in the end, he left without another word. Mike felt like he'd gone fifteen rounds.

He got two things out of that conversation. One, although he still wanted a career once he was done with pandas and togas, he was certain tying his name to Robert Roth's was a great way to ensure that never happened. And, two, he was not nearly as calm about Glinda as he thought he was.

Chapter Thirty

Dehydration headaches were a sure sign she should stop crying, but she couldn't. All evening, all night, and again in the shower. Although now the tears were more from frustration than heartbreak. Her body was out of control, and she couldn't get off her runaway emotional train.

Mike was an asshole. He'd proved it repeatedly. Behind her back. To her face. It wasn't a question.

So why had he defended her to Robert Roth the day before in his trailer?

Glinda hadn't been eavesdropping. Their trailers were right next to each other, and with the windows open and the wind blowing the right way, the conversation had come to her. Not to mention, Roth had never been much for using an inside voice when spewing insults.

Even thinking of Mike playing the good guy set her off on another crying jag.

She thought she was done for the moment when a ringing sounded in her ears. Glinda turned off the water and realized it was a real noise coming from her doorbell. It stopped while she was still in the shower stall, and all she could do was send a "thank you" toward the ceiling for one problem that went away on its own. She needed to find some eye drops to soothe the redness in her eyes, and antihistamines to dry the faucet that was her nose. She was a mess, but nobody else needed to know. She refused to give anyone a single excuse to think they were settling when they worked with her.

"Hello?"

The voice was coming from inside the house. "Dory?"

"I hope so. I'm wearing her pants."

Glinda's terry robe didn't stop a stream of water from trailing behind her as she ran down the hall. "What are you doing here?"

"When your favorite sister calls you in tears two days running because the man of her dreams treats her like some second-place trophy, you call in sick and catch a red-eye. Where else would I be?"

The tears, which had finally trailed off, erupted again. "I'm your only sister."

After a heartening hug, Dory sent her back to finish her shower and promised to have coffee waiting when she got out. Having someone who was undoubtedly on her side and ready to fight for her did wonders. As did the eye drops. Glinda emerged as a woman in control. The illusion was only skin deep, but it was a start. She could fake it till she made it.

Her twin had the common decency to wait until she'd refilled her mug before speaking again. "What are you going to do?"

"I'm going to work this afternoon like I'm supposed to and do my job. It's not like I have any options."

"Call your doctor first. She called twice while you were in the bathroom. Is there something I should know?" Dory's voice was anything but calm, which was frightening. She was supposed to be Glinda's rock.

"Connie called?" Her appointment seemed like a lifetime ago. "Oh. No, nothing to worry about. During my last post-Hawaii adventure appointment, I mentioned I was tired and she ran some blood tests. She wanted to see how low my iron was. The numbers must be back."

"And she'd call twice for that?"

"She would if they were low enough. The labs screwed up, and I had to do the tests again. Crap, I'm going to get an iron shot. I'd rather have a meal of pills than get a shot." A discussion about needles was only slightly better than talking about what had happened with Mike, but she'd take it.

Glinda returned the call to Dr. Booth's office and was put right through. "Is something wrong?"

"I need you to come in," Connie said.

"I've got a two o'clock call time."

"I'll make a space for you in an hour. Make time."

Glinda couldn't argue because Connie was gone. "I have to go in."

"I'll come too. In the meantime, what about Tall, Dark, and Bonehead?"

Glinda tore a strip off a banana and handed it to Dory. Then she did it again and began eating the second one herself. "We only have another twenty days of filming. I can work with him for three weeks. Unless there are script changes, we have one somewhat romantic scene and I'm professional enough to do that."

"I'm sorry, sis."

"Me too. I really liked him." She didn't say she was pretty sure she was in love with him. If she had been, he should have heard the words first.

"What exactly did he do? You weren't clear on the specifics."

"He told me he was settling for me. Because we're both getting older."

"He did not!"

"It gets better. His dad acknowledged I wasn't his first choice for Mike but said I'd do."

"He did not!"

"They both did. Can we continue this in the car?"

Glinda drove to the Barrow Jackson Medical Clinic; Dorothy gawked at the parade of six-figure cars and palm-lined streets. "You can take the girl out of Iowa…" Glinda teased.

"Keep talking, Miss Too-Cool-To-Get-Excited, and I'll tell the nurse to use the big gauge needle in your butt."

"Zipping it."

"Are you sure?" Dory asked.

"About what?"

"About Mike thinking he was settling for you."

"That's what he said."

She could feel Dory's stare weighing on her. They both knew it was one of her hot buttons. "He tried to write it off like he was choosing to settle down with me, but what he said to me and what he said about me were different things."

"And you're sure?" Dory pressed.

"Yes. It's okay. I'll get over it."

It was a fake calm. Glinda knew it. She had created a very thin layer of surface gloss to hide the cracks, but it was holding. She'd have to reapply it hourly because she'd fall to pieces if she didn't keep a constant eye on it. Having Dory beside her helped. Her sister might only be in town for twenty-four hours, but Dory would help her find her balance. By the time she dropped her twin at the airport, she'd be able to stand alone.

Dr. Booth didn't keep her waiting. Connie looked twice at Dory when Glinda introduced her, but didn't ask her to leave. "Your test results came back."

"I gathered. Do I need to have an iron shot?"

"No, and you're pregnant."

"But I don't need a shot?" Then the second half of Connie's statement penetrated. "What?"

"You're pregnant."

"With a baby?"

"Yes, Glinda, you are pregnant with a baby."

She blanked out for a minute. "I'm pregnant."

"Yes, Glinda."

"I'm on the pill."

"It happens."

"Mike used condoms."

"It happens less frequently."

"I'm pregnant with a baby."

"Yes. We need to discuss the next step," Dr. Booth said. It sounded like she wanted to laugh.

"I am so fucked."

"You certainly were," Dory said, her first words in the conversation.

Her favorite sister was going to be very useful at this appointment. Glinda could tell.

Chapter Thirty-One

Things were going too well. He'd had a good night's sleep—the first since Glinda walked out the door, his schedule was running like clockwork, and the tension pervading the production seemed to have lightened.

Even Glinda was acting differently. She'd stared at him that afternoon when she'd arrived on set with her sister. He'd thought something had happened the night before, that she'd come to her senses, or that her twin had somehow talked her around. But they'd rushed to Glinda's trailer without a word to him.

But her look had given him a glimmer of hope.

They hadn't spoken, but not because they were avoiding each other. The sequence coming up had a ton of moving parts, and getting all the players organized within the split-second timing took everyone's full attention.

It didn't stop Glinda from laying her hand on his arm while they were getting into position. "I need to talk to you."

That was all she had time to say. He managed a nod before Antonia ordered them into position. It was hard to shut down the Glinda part of his brain, but the situation ahead needed his full attention.

Dr. Hanzel and Captain Mackenzie were in a shootout with the ninjas. The bad guys thought they had the intrepid duo cornered in an alley, but Jane pulled out a machine gun she'd hidden in her coat and was spraying the alley like she had a never-ending supply of bullets. The first take had been delayed when a production assistant reported a poodle had escaped from a neighboring soundstage and was roaming the studio grounds, but now they had the all-clear.

Antonia called action, and the back-and-forth shooting began. Mike wanted to shake his head; for professional assassins and an army Ranger sniper, the "bullets" never got close.

"Make a break for the car. I'll cover you!" Glinda shouted as she popped up like a whack-a-mole from behind a conveniently located oil barrel.

Mike took his cue, and raced down the alley and around the corner out of sight. Glinda was supposed to follow in thirty seconds. He kept an eye out for her, but something else caught his attention. Something that wasn't supposed to be there.

It was a...he wasn't sure. It looked like a dog, with its lean torso and thin legs, but the coloring was wrong. Its front and back legs were a stark black, in contrast with a white body. Then there was its white head with dark fur around its eyes and ears, and the dripping red stain spreading from the beast's muzzle.

He could see it was a dog as it got closer. It might have been a poodle at some point. Now it was a nightmare. A nightmare which was gaining speed.

As the creature approached, it moved from a bouncy walk to a trot. Then it focused on Mike. The lope broke into a full run, which only brought its bloody mouth into sharper focus.

"Shit," Mike muttered, uncaring of the microphone he wore. There was no place to go. The fake street he was on was a dead end; the only other exit was back through the alley.

He could hear the charging mock-panda growling at him now. There was no camera in the street to record the approach, or his reaction. Judging from the speed at which the crew disappeared, they hadn't planned it as a practical joke either.

"Shit!" he repeated. He gauged the distance and made his decision.

Mike sprinted back into the shot, his college track training rising to the forefront of his mind. He had no time to hesitate. It didn't matter how much his interruption cost, it had to be done. He shouted instructions with the same certainty. "Run!" He grabbed Glinda's arm, pulling her out of position, and dragged her down the narrow passageway.

"What?" She tried to stop him, but he was bigger. And motivated.

He pointed behind him with his free hand. "Run!"

She looked over her shoulder and then started moving. "What is *that*?" she asked.

The actors playing the ninjas also stopped firing. "What *is* that?" one of them yelled before they joined in Mike and Glinda's sprint.

Mike stopped beside one of the two dumpsters against the walls and tossed Glinda onto it. "Keep going," he ordered. She scrambled for the fire escape ladder hanging above it.

Mike jumped onto the hood of the ninja's car, which was parked beside the dumpster. The mutant poodle pounced, paws scrabbling for traction on the metal garbage bin. In the second it took to slide down, Mike joined Glinda on the dumpster. "Up," he said.

They climbed to the third-floor landing, and watched the circus unfold beneath them. Three crew members wrangled the dog into a crate. The camera operator was freaking at the disrupted shot, and Antonia was laughing so hard she had to grip her chair for support.

Glinda crossed her arms on the railing and surveyed the scene with a smile on her face. She looked gorgeous, glowing. He had to admit, it was funny now. He joined her at the rail, his heart pumping wildly. "Do you get the feeling that wasn't in the script?"

"Little bit."

Antonia looked up at them and waved. "You two can come down now. It's going to take some time to get this all sorted, so go do something."

"How about we talk?" Glinda asked Mike.

"We can do that."

Chapter Thirty-Two

They'd barely hit the ground when Antonia told them she'd need more time than she initially said. "I believe the dog is from *America's Best Trained Pet*. I have no idea how such an untrained beast made it past the initial selection process, but we're stuck with it until someone comes to collect it." She rolled her eyes. "I'm starting to feel sympathetic for Lorde and Roth." The woman held her thumb and index finger an inch apart. "A little sympathetic. I know this isn't your fault, but what a disaster." Antonia's smile changed, and it scared Glinda. "It may not be a complete loss."

Mike appeared beside her. "We'll be in my trailer," he said to the director.

It was much nicer than the ones they had in Hawaii. Glinda bit back a smile at the rubber bat Mike had pinned above the door. It wasn't a memento she would have chosen, but it was funny. She took an extra minute to ensure his windows were closed. She didn't want a replay of his conversation with Roth. This would be hard enough without being overheard.

Glinda was too nervous to stand still but she needed to look Mike in the eye. "I was very insulted by something you said. It has recently come to my attention that what I heard has more than one meaning, so if you're willing, I'd like to try to clear things up."

He didn't look impressed, but he didn't order her to leave his trailer either.

She took another look at him, trying to memorize him in case this was as close as she ever got again. He hadn't had a chance to wash off any of his make-up; the powders contoured the strong line of his jaw, and his unmissable cheek bones. His chocolate brown eyes held a hint of sadness that they hadn't before, and she knew she was responsible for it. It wasn't a good feeling.

"On our first date, in the restaurant, you said it was time you settled," Glinda began.

It took forever for him to respond. "Yes."

"Then, at your house, your dad said he was glad you were settling on me."

"I know. I was there."

He didn't get it. He didn't see the insult even when she pointed it out. "If you settle for something, it means it's not your first pick. Settling means accepting inferior things because what you really want isn't available."

Something changed on his face. He was either finally comprehended her point, or was going to let her have it. "Settling is also what you do when you stop running because you realize what's important and you want to keep that goodness in your life," Mike said quietly.

Glinda shook her head. "That's settling down. *Down*," she emphasized. The difference was profound. One meant she was second-best; the other meant she was the reason he didn't have to look for his future anymore, because he'd found it with her. Only the latter was acceptable.

That got a reaction. He rubbed his hand over his head furiously. "You dumped me in front of my family because of semantics?"

"It's not semantics. I've never heard of anyone being happy to settle."

"Glinda, it's an expression."

"*Settling* is what assholes said to my parents when they said they'd have settle for Dorothy being smart instead of pretty like me, which is bullshit because Dory is gorgeous. *Settling* is what directors said to me when they had to settle for body doubles when I refused to waive my no-nudity clause because I was a stuck-up cunt who was probably covered in stretchmarks or needle tracks. *Settling* was—"

"I get it."

He didn't, not really. He couldn't. But he was listening, and now he had a clue as to why it was so important to her. "Then you can see why there is such a huge difference between settling and settling down for me."

"I can understand. What I don't get is why you didn't explain all this at my house?"

God, that was a whole new conversation. She wasn't ready for it, but she couldn't ignore it either. "I'm sorry about that. I wasn't thinking clearly. Will you please accept my apology?"

He didn't make her wait for it. "Yes, Glinda, I'll accept your apology. I'm in love with you! I didn't want you to go in the first place. I'm not going to complain when you come back. Are you back?"

"I'm definitely back."

"Good."

Then, thankfully, he kissed her. He stepped closer, tilted her chin so she met his eyes, and lowered his lips until they met hers. Glinda didn't hold back, she pressed herself into his chest, soaking up all the warmth he offered. She hadn't liked it when she thought he'd been a jerk. She liked him when he was strong and supportive and let her defend herself unless she asked for help. Glinda especially liked him when he kissed her, his scent surrounding her and muffling the rest of the world.

"Are we good?" he asked again. "No more settling, just settling down?"

"Yes."

"Then why are you acting like you still have one foot out the door?"

"I love you too. I want you to know that. But I still need to talk to you," she admitted. Her heart had been breaking a minute ago. Now it was about to explode through her rib cage from a different type of anxiety. She didn't know if she could do it. Maybe it would be better to wait for a couple weeks, let them get their feet back under them again. At least get through principal photography.

"There's more? About settling down?"

"Not about that. That's good. That could be really good. This is about something else."

"Is it bad?"

"Would you work with me again? One on one? Equal co-stars carrying an entire production?" Glinda asked, switching gears.

"In a heartbeat."

"On a long-term project?"

"Still yes."

"For eighteen years or so?" she pressed.

"Eighteen years?"

"I'm pregnant," she blurted.

"But you're on birth control."

"It happens."

"I used condoms."

"It happens less frequently, according to my doctor. I'm definitely pregnant."

The silence was deafening. Her fingers turned white because she was squeezing them together so hard, but she gave him time.

"Pregnant? With a baby?" he asked.

"That's what I said." Mike's eyes widened, and Glinda realized how her comment must have sounded. "I mean literally. I actually said the words 'with a baby' to Doctor Barrow. I know it's a shock. An entirely unexpected, turn your world upside-down shock. I barely believe it myself."

"We're going to have a baby?"

She let loose a breath she hadn't realized she'd been holding. "We are."

Then she was flying, around and around as Mike swept her into his arms and carefully spun her around the tiny living area. "I would love to co-star for the next eighteen years with you."

"Are you sure?"

He set her down without warning. "Stay right there. I mean it." Then he disappeared into the bedroom at the back of the trailer.

She should have known what he'd say. Excepting her colossal semantics mistake, she'd always believed

Mike was one of the good ones. His reaction was more than she'd hoped for. She wasn't excited about being pregnant, not yet. And she didn't not want the baby. She was still working on understanding the situation. But now she was processing the news knowing she wouldn't be doing it alone.

Mike's response was everything.

He returned holding his hand against the side of his leg. "This is almost a week later than I intended to do it, and you may still think it's too soon, but…" He lifted his hand to reveal a black velvet box in his palm.

"I've been ready to settle *down*," he emphasized, "for a while, but the right woman never came along. I wanted somebody smart, and strong, and funny, and who would understand my career. That is a big order to fill. Then these pandas showed up and I discovered this woman I've been working with for years was everything I was looking for. She saved my life, repeatedly, and was amazingly brave, and I didn't have a chance. I know it's fast," he said, raising the lid, "but will you marry me?"

Tears burned in her eyes. She knocked teeth together because she nodded so hard. "Yes. Definitely yes."

After he kissed her—a long while after, because their kiss to seal the deal lasted a second or a lifetime—he rested his forehead against hers. "If everything up until now has been our first movie, I cannot wait to see how the sequel turns out."

"Hollywood ending, Mike. Count on it."

Epilogue

The dress code was formal. Mike straightened his bow tie again. Glinda had knocked it sideways when she'd stolen a kiss just before the limousine had pulled up to the curb. She said he was hotter than she'd ever seen. At eight months pregnant, her libido was running at an all-time high, and it had been revving hot before. He wasn't complaining.

She was stunning in her emerald-tone evening gown. It was fitted at the bust, and the rest was a light flowing fabric that did nothing to hide the swell of her stomach. Her shoes were bedazzled, white flip-flops, which he thought were adorable. Glinda preferred to be done to the nines for special occasions, but her feet hadn't fit inside regular shoes in almost two months. She'd sighed when she put them on before they'd left her house, but they were the only appropriate footwear she had that still fit.

"You look gorgeous."

"I'm not wearing my engagement ring," she complained. "Stupid sausage fingers."

He snagged her hand and raised it to his lips, kissing each fingertip. "I love your fingers."

He wished he could say they'd been inseparable after she told him about what they called their eighteen-year production, but it would have been a lie.

Antonia decided to use the single take of Mike racing back into the shot being chased by the psycho panda-poodle. The *America's Best Trained Pet* escapee became a central figure to *Panda-monium*'s plot, as the original military dog-panda cyborg hybrid that the Chinese ninjas wanted Dr. Hanzel to fix. Mike didn't look at the logic of the script too hard. He was looking forward to seeing the final version; Antonia had been making changes up to the very last minute.

Unfortunately, filming had been the last time he and Glinda had spent any significant time together for months. Glinda was contracted to attend several *Olympus* fan events. Mike had to do a series of photoshoots around the world for Nikolai cologne. He'd missed her third doctor's appointment; they were both upset about that. They settled down quickly at the end of the second trimester, including Mike moving into Glinda's place. She was in a better school district, and her house was better laid out for life with a baby. Five months later, things were getting better every day.

"Okay, I'm ready, but as soon as we get inside I'm hitting the bathroom."

Camera flashes and shouted questions greeted them from the moment the opened the car door. Antonia Caruso was further up the red carpet, with Rio Rodrigues halfway between them. Mike and Glinda hadn't risen to the "power couple" level but they'd had their fair share of media exposure, especially once Glinda started to show.

While making the movie had been a challenge, the media rounds to drum up interest for its release had been a riot. The interviewers had given them a lot of grief about the plot, but since he and Glinda showed up with various outtakes that left audiences in stitches, everyone seemed willing to come on board and give *Panda-monium* a try.

To remind people of the real star of the movie, Amanda the Panda—returned to working order—was sitting on a pedestal, waving to attendees entering the theater. Her minions, various humans in cartoon-like panda costumes, ran around revving up the crowd.

One man-panda in particular was thrilling the onlookers with cartwheels and back flips. Mike had no idea how the costume's head was still attached. Rio came back to join them and watch the show.

Mike knew the second the acrobatic bear saw them. He jumped three feet straight in the air, twice, and took off running.

Mike did a quick calculation. Mass, velocity, distance, required deceleration space. The answer was he and Glinda were going to be bowled over by an overenthusiastic cartoon.

Mike gently pushed Glinda into Rio's arms and turned to face the oncoming juggernaut. He thought his aggressive stance would cause the other man to slow down, but the panda-man didn't break pace. He reached for Mike.

Mike grabbed his attacker's elbow with one hand and pulled him close. He reached around and put his other hand on the man's back. He pulled on the arm at the same time as he thrust out his hip, and the panda-man flew through the air and landed flat on his back.

The crowd burst into applause at the stunt. Mike smiled and waved, and bent to help the other man up. "If you ever try to jump a pregnant lady again, I'll let Glinda deal with you. Did you hear about the offer she made to our director? Left or right?" he asked in a quiet voice.

The other man nodded.

"If this happens again, to anyone, I'll tell her you said both."

The actor's paw-covered hand moved to cover his groin. He accepted Mike's help to his feet, bounced twice as he waved to the crowd, and raced off.

"What was that all about?" Glinda asked without letting her smile slip.

"A tip for future acting gigs."

"You okay?"

"It takes more than a panda to take me down," he said.

Glinda froze. He didn't understand why until he saw the *Hollywood 24/7* camera in front of them. "It takes more than a panda to take you down?" she repeated, a little louder than necessary. "Because I'm pretty sure—"

"Spoiler alert!" he shouted in mock exasperation. "Let them see the movie first."

She huffed. Her puffed-out cheeks and slight flush make him weak in the knees. Her beauty astounded him every time. The look she returned when he grinned at her said she felt the same way. "Fine, I guess I can hold off for another two hours."

"Is it true you are already planning a sequel to *Panda-monium*?" a reporter shouted.

Antonia and the studio had prepared an announcement for the premiere about a proposed sequel, but he hadn't realized the news was already out. He informed them that he was more than willing, so long as he got to work with Glinda again—and if they got more input into the production side of things. Considering how badly things had gone, and that he and Glinda were the last two original members standing, it wasn't hard to get them to agree.

"It is."

"Do you know the name of it yet?"

He smiled at the ridiculous working title that Zubov, Ackerman, and Zano had come up with. "I do." He paused, because he had to get it right. Glinda squeezed his arm, and he nodded so they could make the announcement together.

"*Llama-ssacre.*"

THE END

ABOUT ELLE RUSH

Elle Rush is a contemporary romance author from Winnipeg, Manitoba, Canada. When she's not travelling, she's hard at work writing books which are set all over the world. From Hollywood to the house next door, her heroes will make you sigh and her heroines will make you laugh out loud.

Elle has a degree in Spanish and French, barely passed German, and is learning Italian and Filipino. She flunked poetry in every language she ever studied. She also has mild addictions to tea, her garden, bad sci-fi movies (hello, *Sharknado* fan!) and HGTV.

For the latest updates on Elle's books, please check out her website and sign up for her free newsletter at www.ellerush.com/newsletter, or follow her on Facebook or Twitter.

Other Books

HOLLYWOOD TO OLYMPUS
Screen Idol
Drama Queen
Leading Man
It Girl
Action Hero

NORTH POLE UNLIMITED
Decker & Joy
Hollis & Ivy
Nick & Eve

RESORT ROMANCES
Cuban Moon
Mexican Sunsets
Dominican Stars
Mayan Midnights

STAND ALONE
Private Encore

www.ingramcontent.com/pod-product-compliance
Lightning Source LLC
Chambersburg PA
CBHW070833120626
46556CB00002B/740